Leading Ladies

10 Powerful Ladies Sharing Life's Lessons & Leaving A Legacy For Other Powerful Ladies

Compiled By

Distinction Publishing House

Published by Distinction Publishing House
Dover, Denver, Colorado
United States of America
www.distinctionpublishinghouse.com

ISBN: 979-8-9894214-7-3

This book is printed on acid-free paper.

Printed in the United States of America

Acknowledgements

Distinction Publishing House is immensely grateful for the unwavering support, dedication, and inspiration that have fueled the creation of this book.

To the incredible Leading Ladies featured:
Acribba J. Lightbourne, Simmone L. Bowe, Holly Riley-Woodside, Sherry Johnson Deal, Lauren-Ashley Heastie, Sherell Brown, Sandena Neely, Juliet Seymour, Jovita Charite, and Deborah Basden, Thank you!

Yes, thank you Leading Ladies for sharing your stories, wisdom, and experiences with honesty and courage. Your strength, resilience, and trailblazing spirit are a testament to the transformative power of women's leadership.

Special thanks to family, friends, and associates for their unwavering encouragement, belief in Distinction Publishing House's vision, and patience throughout the writing process. Your love and support have been our anchors during this incredible journey.

Lastly, to the readers of this book, thank you for embarking on this empowering and transformative voyage with us. May the stories within these pages ignite your passion, inspire your ambitions, and fuel your drive to lead with purpose, courage, and grace.

Dedication

*"To the trailblazers, the visionaries, and the fearless
Leading Ladies who inspire us all"*

This book is dedicated to Leading Ladies and all those who have
shaped history, broken barriers, and left an indelible
mark on the world.

Your resilience, determination, and unwavering courage have
paved the way for generations of powerful women to follow
in your footsteps.

Your legacy is a beacon of light for all aspiring, powerful ladies,
showing them the boundless possibilities that await when they
embrace their potential and push beyond limits.

Table of Contents

Introduction

Through the captivating stories of these ten Leading Ladies, readers will discover the secrets behind their success, the obstacles they overcame, and the valuable lessons they learned along the way.

From trailblazers in business, education, government, healthcare, communications, religion, to leaders within the community and diplomacy, this book highlights the diverse achievements of remarkable women making a difference in various fields.

The coming chapters provide unique perspectives and personal anecdotes, allowing readers to connect with the featured Leading Ladies intimately. Their stories will ignite inspiration, encourage self-belief, and motivate readers to fulfil their potential. As they are true testaments to the power of resilience, determination, and the unyielding spirit of women.

However, it does not stop there. This book goes beyond the achievements and focuses on the legacy these Leading Ladies are leaving behind. They share their insights, wisdom, and life lessons to empower other women to take charge of their lives, embrace their strengths, and pursue their dreams fearlessly. No matter where you are on your journey, this book is a beacon of light, reminding you that you too can make a difference.

Whether you dream of becoming a CEO, an artist, a community leader, or something entirely unique, these Leading Ladies have paved the way and will guide you towards success.

Chapter 1
Acribba J. Lightbourne
"Purpose, Faith, Timing"

As I write this reflection of my life, I think of you, my sisters, and other young and upcoming women of tomorrow. The life lessons that I have learned through trial and error are my gifts to you.

My parents always told me that I was a special child. Every year on my birthday, my mother would show me my navel string as a reminder of the miracle surrounding my birth. She had experienced complications during delivery and was given the option of saving herself or me. Unselfishly, she chose to let me live, and she lived as well despite the odds. Well, some 43 years later, she and I are still together. What a Mighty God!

Your Words Have Power!

During childhood, I often said that when I grew up, I would have a fairy-tale wedding in a fluffy white dress with a diamond crown that looked just like a doll my father had given me. My future looked bright until, at the age of 19, I married a man I had only known for eight months.

While preparing for the wedding, I discovered I was pregnant. As I had said, I wore the Cinderella gown with a crown on my wedding day and later gave birth to a beautiful baby girl who looked exactly like my doll.

My childhood words had manifested in the physical. However, I quickly learned that fairy tales were an illusion. My childhood fantasy had become a nightmare from which I could not be awakened. My husband abused me emotionally, mentally, and physically. Life and death are in the power of the tongue, and the words you speak will determine the trajectory of your life.

Take Responsibility For Your Decisions

As women, we are very emotional beings and believe the lie that if we are not in a relationship, something is wrong with us. After divorcing my then-husband, I immediately entered another relationship with someone younger than me.

This relationship was also filled with torment, abuse, and pain. Moreover, I was arrested, thrown on the floor, handcuffed and placed in a cold cell one night. I faced trial and possible imprisonment for something I did not do. During that time, I was the Vice President of my family's business, so the arrest brought disgrace to my family.

Nevertheless, the night I was arrested was a turning point in my life. I had an encounter where I heard someone singing, "Tis so sweet to trust in Jesus". Feeling like the biggest failure, I wept over my mistakes. I was broken, hurt, and suffering from low self-esteem. Prior to the arrest, I had deserted my daughter, who was failing school and experiencing emotional pain. I needed to make it right. But how?

One day, I got in my car, and it was as if an angel drove me to a counselling centre. I wanted to get my life in order and regain my daughter's trust. My life turned around after I confessed, admitted my wrongs, and took responsibility. I left that relationship and made the best decision: I gave my life and heart to God.

Wait On God's Timing

Fast forward, I became CEO of the family business. God did that and blew my mind because I did not feel worthy. I believed my past would have always defined me, but God removed the stains and made everything new.

Then, after a year and six months of not dating, the man God designed for me found me. I was not looking for a relationship then, and marriage was far from my mind.

A year later, he proposed, and the following year, we were married. I prayed for guidance because I did not want to repeat the failed relationship cycle. I submitted myself to God's will, and He made it clear that it was

His will for my life and ministry. The favour of God was evident in both of our lives. God truly carved my husband out of the pages of His book for me.

Hold On To Your Faith

We decided to have a baby, but I discovered my tubes were blocked and needed removal. I was devastated, but my husband assured me we would do whatever was necessary to have a baby, leading us to try in vitro fertilization (IVF).

God put my faith to the test. I wanted a child, and He wanted a sacrifice. He wanted to see if I truly depended on Him. For inspiration, I was referred to the 'War Room' movie, where I learned about going to war with the real enemy - Satan.

After watching the movie, I stuck pictures of things I desired around my home. I found a resting place under my staircase and placed prayers and pictures on the wall. Unknown to me, I had erected something sacred known as an "ALTAR," just as Jacob did when he poured the oil upon the rock after having a vision of the ladder where angels ascended and descended. I dedicated the space to God and called it Bethel, "Where He dwells." It was the only place I found peace. My sacrifice was the altar that would alter the enemy's plans.

Our journey to conceive was a time of great faith and favour, and we were able to cover the exorbitant cost miraculously. As Christmas neared, I told God I only desired to carry a child that year. I promised Him I would share my story if He gave me that. Just before the holidays, I became pregnant on 14th December, 2015 – the best gift ever. But I endured my pregnancy privately.

The day of delivery was the first time I authorized the hospital to give me a blood transfusion. After a safe C-section delivery, Skylar Faith was born. But I began bleeding out because my doctor could not stitch the incision. My life was in danger, and I needed emergency surgery. Although there was panic around me, I felt peace.

I believed God would not abandon me after bringing me that far. I came out ALIVE. My doctor confessed that if no one knew who God was they met Him that day. God used my life to prove His sovereignty over situations. Years later, I realized that I relived my mother and father's experiences during my birth. I decided by the power in my tongue to curse that cycle in the name of Jesus and declared that my daughters shall not relive that curse. It would be broken and end with me.

Your Life Has Purpose

God wanted my whole heart to fulfil His purpose for my life. Out of this experience, my ministry, Finding Faith Ministries International, was birthed, opening the way for one of the fastest-growing talk shows named Faith Talk, a clothing line called Faith Line, and Prayer & Bible Club.

Yes, God knew me, and you, before we were formed in our mother's womb and called us to purpose. When you trust Him, He will give you beauty for ashes.

Chapter 2
Simmone L. Bowe

"The Winding Way to Purpose

"Not all those who wander are lost."
J. R. R. Tolkien

I've often felt that I spent too much of my life wandering, figuring things out, losing my way, and making mistakes. It is almost as if you see the sands of time slipping through your fingers and, before you know it, you are in your fifties grasping desperately at the grains. Sadly, you cannot turn the hourglass over in real life. All you can do is make the most of the time you have left and embrace the fact that everything that has happened has come to teach you, shape you, and move you closer to your destiny. In fact, even though you may feel lost, you are exactly where you should be.

What is My Why?

When I was younger, I would secretly envy those people who seemed to have their lives mapped out so clearly. They would know exactly what they wanted to do in their careers and how they wanted their personal lives to look. Meanwhile, I had no idea of what I wanted my life to look like. It was as if I was walking each day in a fog, groping in front of me as I took shaky steps forward, searching, longing. In the darkness, I grabbed at things that looked like the hazy outline of a guidepost. Sometimes it took me forward, sometimes backwards, and sometimes sideways. What is it going to take to get on track?

I graduated from high school at the tender age of fifteen without a clue about what I wanted to do next. I did not have a leaning toward anything specific. I had friends who were so sure of what they wanted to study – law, medicine, business, and writing. My courses were very general, at the advice of my guidance counsellor, so I did a bit of everything: English Language, English Literature, Mathematics, Spanish, French, Geography, Biology, Typing, and Computer Applications.

Now faced with making a major decision at a young age, I asked my father for advice. He suggested that I try hospitality. We had a local hospitality school, and I signed up. That was one of the best decisions of my life. I fell in love with the hospitality industry and excelled in my studies. This started a winding path to hotel life, university abroad and the world of work, life and love. As much as it felt like I was lost, I was right on track for a wild ride.

Leading Lady Lessons Learned:

1. You will not always have a clear picture of your purpose at a young age. It is important to have the freedom to explore possibilities until you get that inner nudge;
2. It is okay to ask for help; and
3. It is a blessing when you have people in your life who give you good advice. Embrace it.

Work, Work, Work, Work, Work

My first job was in my father's tour operator company. I would go along with my oldest sister to the airport where she would go to meet flights, assist passengers onto my dad's buses, and transport them to their hotel. I was too young to get involved in that side of it, so I busied myself doing one of my favourite things: answering the phone! The taxi and tour bus driver nicknamed me 'Operator' and I took my job seriously!

When I turned sixteen and started hospitality school, my dad, and sister asked me to conduct a training session in customer service with their tour desk representatives. Me at sixteen, with zero knowledge of teaching or training accepted the challenge and was told I did a great job. Little did I know it would spark a love for teaching and corporate training that became an indelible part of my life to this day.

My mother was an educator, so books and music always surrounded us growing up. She always made sure we were active in church and youth activities. These are the foundation of a thriving, learning community and a growth mindset. Church folk have a way of fully affirming you no matter what you try and when you couple that with a supportive family and village, you cannot go wrong.

I sometimes wonder if I got too much affirmation growing up because by the time I hit my upper teens and early twenties, life started to hit hard. After I finished university at twenty, I returned home hopeful and ready to contribute to my community. My first stop at job hunting was at the hospitality school, where I graduated at the top of my class. I figured this would be easy.

I set up an appointment with the Executive Director who knew me well. I received the Executive Director's Award at graduation and even a job offer on the night of the ceremony. As I sat in his office and shared my dream to return to the school as a teacher, I was not prepared for his response. He said, "You are not well-rounded enough to teach here. You need to travel the world a bit and come back with some experience."

I was dumbfounded. Is this man serious? I was fresh out of university, an education my parents paid for first of all, so I do not have any 'travel around the world' money. It is time to work. He was not budging, and I left his office feeling deflated and dejected. Now what?

I reflected on what else I was good at and thought, "Maybe I can be a journalist. I love writing." So, I applied to one of the local newspapers for a journalist's position. Looking back, I realized how green and naïve I was. I had no idea of workplace politics or the nuances of our society that had some unspoken rules of what you can do and where you can go. That newspaper company was one of them.

My father was a politician before he ventured into hospitality and management consulting. In a small community, he was very visible, as well as what he stood for and who he stood with politically. What I did not know was that the newspaper was on the other side of the political fence. I went through all the initial requirements of the application – a test, a sample article that was published, and finally, I had an interview with the managing editor and owner. After asking my name, she asked me point blank: "Who is your people?" In The Bahamas, that translates to "tell me who your family is." I told her my father's name and the rest, as they say, was history. Despite my sample article being published without an edit, I never got a call back from them. Again, I asked, "Now what?"

I attended the Anglican Church at the time and somehow I got wind that they were looking for an English teacher. I built up the courage to go for it and applied. This time, the Director of Education for the Anglican Schools decided to take a chance on me and I got the job. Amid my excitement, she cautioned me with words that slapped me in the face. She admonished me, "Don't take your St. Andrew's School snobbishness to my school!" I looked at her blankly and did not respond. I could not respond. What did she mean? I am not a snob and never have been snobbish. My parents came from humble beginnings and never forgot their roots and made sure their children were very grounded.

I was hurt and confused by her statement. It was my first taste of being judged, diminished, and falsely accused just because I was privileged enough to attend one of the best schools on the island.

She was not the first older woman to hurt me professionally. I can recall being in interviews for other jobs as I sought to advance my career, where I would be openly insulted and my integrity questioned. While I tried not to be bitter, I was gravely disappointed that older professional women did not seem to be open to moulding and mentoring young professional women at all.

In fact, it seemed that they kept career advancement tightly guarded for 'their own' – family, children of their friends, or people who would be blindly loyal and submissive to them. This was a harsh lesson, and I vowed that I would never want to be like them. Though I longed for a mentor,

I made sure that I was a willing and nurturing mentor to up-and-coming professionals. I became a supporter and advocate for the underdog in society, and smoothly transitioned into a career in human resources. As much as I could, I held the door open for others. Often it was behind the scenes, coaching and mentoring, training and advising others who stood in their own right, shining brightly in their fields.

Leading Lady Lessons Learned:

- ✓ Say yes to every opportunity to learn and grow professionally;
- ✓ Not everyone will be a fan or supporter. Keep trying anyway; and
- ✓ Let the pain of rejection and betrayal help you to grow into a better person.

As a "Leading Lady" yourself, be very intentional about finding your why. Life may take you on a complex path to discover it, but do not give up. Knowing your purpose will give you clarity on your next move. Your purpose will help you to define and refine who you really are. Your purpose will shape your boundaries of acceptable behaviours, habits, and choices. Most of all, your purpose will give your life a deep, authentic sense of meaning and value because everything you do will be aligned with the core of who you really are.

No more hiding, no more running, no more dummying down, no more being disrespected. Why? When you stand in your purpose, in your true identity, and in your essence, you are unapologetically you — a leading lady leaving a legacy of grit, grace, and greatness.

Chapter 3
Holly Riley-Woodside
"Are You Woman Enough?"

One of my biggest struggles was wondering if I was good enough as a daughter, as a mother, as an employee, as a wife, and most of all, as a woman. There are so many roles we play as women that sometimes it is so easy to become lost in the expectations of others.

I always wanted to keep the peace, be nice, lead by example and be the bigger person. As a daughter, I was so torn, trying so hard to receive love and attention from my dad felt nearly impossible. It was as if everything and everyone else were more important than I was.

As a child, I grew up only seeing my parents occasionally. That was hard! Even though it might have seemed like the best option sometimes as parents we need to think longer and harder. As a mother, the thing that gave me drive was my childhood experiences. I never wanted my children to feel the way I felt growing up - my parents one way and my siblings the other. I grew up with family, but I yearned for my family. It seemed like everyone close to me betrayed me.

My life was one big hurdle after the next. My career was one of the areas that I had the most control over. I chose my career path, and I loved what I did. Being able to help guide young minds and hopefully change their lives for the better by allowing them to explore their options and to teach and show them that they could be anything that they wish as long as they put in the work.

My hardest journey was my role as a wife. You could never really be prepared for an experience such as that. Your flame flickers so bright in the beginning, but as time passes, you begin to experience things, see things, and hear things.

One of the easiest things to do is to listen to people's advice, but to put it into practice is another story. I told someone the other day no one goes into a marriage wishing or hoping it will fail. When you get married to a person, you commit to being in it forever. No wife wishes harm and failure on their spouse.

If men only knew the amount of prayer a wife goes on her knees to pray for protection for her family. Between the heart and the eyes, I do not know which one got tortured the most. During these times of trials, I felt lost, burdened, and hopeless. I always needed to know why. I wanted to understand why I was getting hurt so much. Why was everything so hard?

Growing up, I had to figure out many things for myself. For years, I would beg my mom to drop me by my dad on the weekend. I just wanted to be around him. I loved my dad and wanted to make him so proud. But he did not see me! My Mom tried to shelter me from the disappointments, but I was too determined to be around him.

I will never forget my Aunt she was always there for me. She was so sweet and nice. I cannot remember her even raising her voice except to call me from across the road at my cousin Chavara's house. There was a time when I went to my dad's and the way he carried on with me, I promised I would never go back there. I remember writing him a long, long, letter and leaving it where he could find it. If I wanted to visit anyone, I would visit my aunt and that was it. My Mom left the country and my dad, well he never really saw me!

I was very fortunate to have Vy in my life. She taught me to be humble, kind and mannerly. It was these traits that I used to help me in this journey called life.

I worshipped my mom. She played all the sports. She was a fearless, beautiful woman, and I wanted to be fearless, just like her. I went to all of her games. I was always ready to go with her. I would sit for hours waiting for her to pick me up.

I remember I got my test results, and I was so excited to tell her, but the only thing she said was "Mmmmmm." That rocked me to my core. I was trying to show her how well I did, so she could be proud of me.

When my mom left the country, that hurt and afterwards I would sit for hours waiting for her to show up, but she never did. Sometimes, as parents, we must make choices that we may not be proud of, and sometimes there is no way to say what needs to be said.

As parents, we hurt our children, and we hurt them badly. I was never a disrespectful child, but I always did as I was told. But as I grew, I realised that some choices just needed to be made. But as a mother, am I doing everything possible that I can do for my kids?

At a very early age, I realized that if I wanted to improve my lifestyle, I had to work hard at it now. My family did not have the money to put me through college. I had to use my education to help me. I kept my grades up and passed my national exams to qualify for a scholarship in education.

I was going through a very hard time in grade 11 and my guidance counsellor at the time listened to me. She guided me, reassured me and gave me the motivation I needed to decide what it was I wanted to do with my life.

I was so impressed by her that I decided to become an educator. I wanted to make a difference in the lives of others. However, this journey was not without its many challenges.

I started with my Bachelor's degree in education and then I did my Master's degree in school counselling and guidance. At one point, I tried so hard to get into guidance and I was constantly being turned down.

One year I prayed. I said, "Lord I will not push the issue because you are in charge." I left the situation to God. He knows best, and he will do better.

Driven by the reality that my future depended on what I engaged in, what I allowed to distract me would make or break me, I could not allow myself to be distracted. My activities as a teenager consisted of school, church, and home. Most activities happened on Saturday and that was church time, from Bible School in the morning to AY (Adventist Youth) in the evening until sunset.

As I look back on these times, I am appreciative because I grew to know the Lord in a personal way. Sometimes as kids, you need to just shut up and listen to your parents. I thought I was missing a world of stuff, but there was zero tolerance for missing church.

If I am being honest with myself, I can say that it made me a better and stronger young lady. Growing up doing what I had to do, not what I wanted to do, moulded me to be more disciplined and focused. Not to mention, I was not easily distracted by teasing and bullying.

I had classmates who travelled every weekend, who wore the best brand of clothing and always had money. What was provided was what I had to accept, and I was humbled by that. I was able to graduate second in my class and obtained the Ministry of Education Scholarship Grant under the leadership of Mrs. Edith Rolle. I was blessed to have ladies like Mrs. Cheryl Carey and Mrs. Jennifer Symonette, who assisted me during my tenure at the College of The Bahamas. There were times when I had no food, but I got through that.

My biggest hurdle came when I got pregnant with my daughter. There were family members who said I would "Never make it, I was finished!" But I pushed through; I used them as my motivation to get back in school and finish.

I worked, took care of my daughter, and went back to school. I knew that I could have sent my baby home to Andros and then go back to school, but I always remembered how I felt when my mom left. I did not want my baby to experience that, so I kept her with me. I had made the decision that led to having a child, so it was my responsibility to take care of her.

Our lives become much more bearable when we can honestly take responsibility for our actions and not blame others. It was rough I kid you not, but I learned to focus on the outcome.

Growing up, I never wanted my kids to experience the pain I felt as a child, so as a mother, I always made sure my kids' needs were met. However, three years into my career, my daughter got sick. She was diagnosed with Wilms tumour and was in the fourth stage. This is a childhood cancer of the kidneys. There are barely any signs or symptoms, so it is almost undetectable.

I was posted at Fresh Creek Primary, at the time. I had to take the next flight out of Andros because her stomach was swollen so big. I was devastated. My mom told me to take her to the United States of America, and I did.

My life was never the same. I devoted everything to making sure my daughter was comfortable and happy. There were times I would have to leave Jackson Memorial Hospital and walk on 20th Street just to cry. I could not allow her to see me cry.

Dionnete lost both of her kidneys; she had a bone marrow transplant and multiple surgeries along with chemo and radiation. I was told that she would not be able to have kids because the radiation was extensive. I have never cried so much; I have never felt so lost! But what could I do?

I could not give up. This was my child! I spent countless months and days in the Hospital. The Hospital was all that she knew. As a mother, I felt every needle, every procedure.

There were times when I had to hold her down or help strap her down just to allow the doctors to give her a needle. It was after her kidney transplant that I had to force her to walk and eat. Watching my child experience pain after pain caused me pain.

Dionnete had a kidney transplant and the kidney had to be removed because of infections. Years later, she was on dialysis three times a week and waiting on a kidney transplant, but we had no money to afford it. But how as a mother did I keep her hopeful and happy?

I was torn between being a mother and a wife. There were many times I questioned my worth and allowed many situations to repeat that I should have stopped during the early onset. But during those hard times, I turned to God. Sometimes I did not even know what to pray for, but in the end, I asked the Lord to let His will be done!

The embarrassment and disrespect that I faced weighed deep down inside of me to where I lost sight of who I was. For years, I was on autopilot. The amount of power we give men because we love them can literally cause harm to us. People had to have been praying for me.

There were times when I got off from work I would drive across to The Curry (a beach area) strip down to my undies, go in the sea and cry. I would cry and talk to God after a long time. I would put on my clothes and drive home.

There were times when I was having dizzy spells and did not know why. Stress is one of the leading killers in the world. I was prepared to go head-on against anything or anyone for my marriage if we did it together. I wanted to be his Bonnie and him to be my Clyde, but easier said than done.

People can only do to you what you allow them to do. The disrespect is partially your fault because you never took a stand. The realization of this hurt so badly. I was trying to figure out how I got to this point. When did things change so drastically? But we see what we want to see.

There are people in your life who will judge you, mistreat you, and write you off, but then there is a small handful who will be there to shake you until every bad thought, negative energy and sign of doubt are shaken out of you. I was able to forgive my mom because I realized if she had not left me and gone to live in the USA, I would not have been able to take my daughter there for medical assistance. I could never repay her for the things she is doing for my child.

I am constantly evaluating myself, trying to improve myself and trying to be the best version of myself there is. In all of my roles, as a daughter, mother, employee, wife and woman, I have done my endeavour best. But no one can tell you when to be done and what decisions to make.

You cannot force anyone to love you, but you can love yourself and know your worth. In the end, you will have peace of mind and those who love you will always love you. Be you and be the best you there will ever be! You are, we are, imperfectly perfect.

Chapter 4
Sherry Johnson Deal

"The Forerunner & The Closed Doors"

"If God Closes A Door, He Will Open Another"

In every generation, God destines a forerunner to be born into a family to take on the mammoth task of breaking generational curses. This task, although weighty, when carried out, is purposed to ultimately rewrite the course of history for generations to come.

Although this assignment from God should be viewed as a privilege and an inspiration for others to follow, the magnitude of it comes with its fair share of fights, struggles, sleepless nights, rejections, and closed doors. When we consider all this, one would become weary and question God's divine plan.

One will often question if the stress of breaking barriers is really worth it. One may ask, "Why should I be the one to endure suffering to facilitate this so-called 'rite of passage' for family members, who in certain instances, I may not know or honestly dislike?" "Why should I be the sacrificial lamb and pay the price so that others could elevate to levels of success I would have once conquered and without so much sweat?" The simple answer is - because God has chosen you!

Yes, He has handpicked you from the foundation of the world to do what others could not do in their generation. However, the reassurance for the forerunner is that God's grace, which often accompanies trials and tribulations, is sufficient for you and will undergird you.

Just like many others, you were equipped with all the capabilities needed to run your own race and finish strong. It is never easy when adversity shows up unannounced and you are ill-prepared prepared. Rest assured, however, that the fire in the furnace will ignite the leader in you to overcome and be victorious. What was meant to destroy you will build character development - the key needed to open new doors.

In April 2021, I was deployed to work in the United States of America. In the eyes of my counterparts, this posting, like many others, was considered as one of the highest honours in one's diplomatic career. Apart from the immunities and privileges that came with this assignment, the joy and fulfilment of representing one's country, serving its diaspora, assisting visitors, and engaging in investor relations were some of the many highlights to look forward to.

With much zeal and enthusiasm, I kept in view the weight of the appointment and took pride in same. What was a truly merited and properly earned appointment predestined for an auspicious end suffered the inglorious and unfair fate of a premature disruption at the hands of a vile superior who in his disingenuous orchestration and machinations, had wilfully elected to misinterpret, misapprehend and disregard my statutory role in providing policy guidance.

Although having served and served well, a series of unceremonious treatment ensued. I was barred from the Office as a result and had no opportunity to pack up my belongings. I was told that my belongings would be packed and shipped to The Bahamas. Most unfortunately, the Office turned off my mobile phone service, requested the US Department of State to deactivate my credentials, and locked my e-mail (which did not allow me time to say my goodbyes and wind down my professional affairs). I was told to return the Office laptop at an undisclosed location despite having been given three additional months by the Ministry of Foreign Affairs, Headquarters in The Bahamas, to wind down my affairs in the United States of America.

The news coupled with the unfair treatment, impacted my health significantly. My blood pressure escalated through the roof. I had severe headaches and was confined to my bed because of depression and mental fatigue.

What was disheartening about this process was the lack of intervention by the Ministry's Headquarters in The Bahamas. As it relates to my recall, or any recall in fact, protocols, policies, and procedures are put in place to ensure a seamless transition to one's country of origin. In my situation, they were disregarded.

It felt as though this superior was above impunity. The question to be answered was "Why?" "Why did he conduct himself as though he was free from consequences for his actions?" "Why was there an absence of professionalism in this recall process?"

On the other hand, why didn't the then Permanent Secretary at Headquarters intervene, or better yet, why didn't he issue a scathing rebuke to stop the snowball of mistreatments? I along with other high-ranking Government Officials requested that my mobile phone be turned on and the e-mail be reinstated so that I could properly wind down my work affairs, but the Permanent Secretary never directed this so-called 'superior' to do the same, at least that is how it seemed. The Permanent Secretary's response to my recall was "I am a creature of instruction." This would have suggested that someone of a higher rank instructed this recall. Could it have been the Political Directorate? Was it political victimization? Hmm. You be the judge.

What sparked these thoughts of political victimization was the fact that, as a career diplomat and non-political appointee, I was deployed abroad under the Free National Movement (FNM) in 2021. The deployment in 2021 was essentially to right the wrongs of being recalled in 2018, because the then Head of Mission believed that I was a Progressive Liberal Party (PLP) supporter. Now serving under the PLP administration, I was rumoured to be an FNM. Well, help me Howard! As one would say in The Bahamas, "Ya can't win for losing." By way of information, the PLP and FNM are political parties that have rivalled each other since "time immemorial" in The Bahamas.

How were these conclusions drawn? I am apolitical. I serve the agenda of the Government of the day. I was instrumental in helping hundreds of Bahamians in distress and visitors alike, channelling multimillion-dollar investment opportunities to the Capital. Throughout the years, I contributed significantly to national development and consequently, in 2021, received from Project Bahamas the top female Millennial Award in the categories of education, diplomacy and as a change agent. Everyone who knows me well knows that I sincerely despise politics.

In my opinion, it is a dirty game filled with empty promises, corruption, victimization and the likes. So, tell me why was I caught up in a political whirlwind? Why couldn't the "powers that be" see the value I brought to the Government in the international arena? Why couldn't the powers that be simply view me as a career diplomat and nothing more? Why treat me like a terrorist, like I committed treason?

Here is another possible reason why - it was because certain officers within the Foreign Ministry, because of coveting my post, began to manufacture lies to have me removed. I did my investigation and discovered that it was officers that I once worked closely with – all who were desperately seeking an opportunity abroad, and by any means necessary. Even if it meant taking down someone and that someone was me.

What was not surprising, however, was that every one of them, after eventually being posted abroad, was recalled after a short period. When I tell you, KARMA has no expiration date. Truer words have never been spoken. Men fail to realize that what you sow, you reap. How you enter a space will be exactly how you leave it. You get what you deserve in the end. The truth always prevails, even though it takes a little longer to make its rounds. Vindication!

After the three–month period had ended, I made my way to The Bahamas. I moved in with my mom and brother. My mother at this time was challenged medically with several ailments including dementia, hypertension, and type 2 diabetes. She needed love, attention, and specialized care. To this end, I took the time to cater to and care for her.

My personal life took a standstill, given the fact that I, along with my brother, were my mother's caretakers by default. I was able to administer her medication, cook food, wash her clothes, prepare her clothes for church and take her to several agencies to receive medical treatment and social services, among other things. Although emotionally taxing at times, it was worth it.

Fast forward to 2023 in July. My mother succumbed to her illness and died on one of the most significant days in Bahamian history – Independence – 10th July. Not only was this day significant for thousands of Bahamians, but the date within itself for my mother symbolized her freedom from sickness and the stresses of this life.

However, the months leading up to her transition, although filled with medical challenges, were most enjoyable. We were able to spend quality mother-daughter time together – going to church, grocery shopping, stamp collecting, walking in the park, eating good food, dancing and watching movies. In hindsight, what I thought was a devastating closed door of posting abroad, which brought about elevating emotional stress, turned out to be God directing me to provide care for my beloved mother during her last eight months on this earth. My Mom desperately needed my help, and the recall worked out in both of our favour because trying to care for her overseas would have been challenging.

Lessons Learnt

I can provide you with countless examples of how God permitted closed doors in my life, and yes, unexpectedly. At the time of their closing, there was immense pain, disappointment and a myriad of emotions that accompanied what I deemed were negative human experiences. However, I learnt to keep in view that God did not permit doors to close without redirecting me to new doors of possibilities, purpose and fulfilment.

The best part of the undeserved recall, however, was the valuable lesson of discerning times and seasons. This lesson was instrumental for me to navigate the new door. I realized that my mother had limited time on the planet and she needed to redeem the time – as brief as it was. Despite the door being closed on the mother-daughter experience, I was now presented with opportunities for personal and spiritual development and a much-needed focus on health and wellness.

My mother, on the other hand, was now free from sickness, disease, and the cares of this world. She was now enjoying an incorruptible, celestial body, and abiding in the arms of Christ – her Saviour. Nothing, no one and no prolonged time on this earth could compare to that!

I would leave you with these words of wisdom. When faced with closed doors, it is important to remember that every challenge presents opportunities for growth and reflection. One must learn to unlock the lessons that come with every twist and turn in life's journey.

Here are several takeaways to consider:

1. **Embrace Change:** When a door closes, it is a sign that change is on the horizon. Embrace the unknown and trust that God has a better plan where new opportunities will emerge;

2. **Know That Vindication Is Your Portion:** If men close the door to bring about shame, disgrace, and harm, God will right the wrongs and reward the perpetrators with their just reward in His time;

3. **Reflect & Learn:** Use this moment to reflect on experiences and glean valuable lessons. Every closed door is a chance to learn and grow – character development;

4. **Pivot & Adapt:** Instead of focusing on what is lost, pivot your perspective towards what could be gained. Adaptability is key in navigating life's difficulties; and

5. **Stay Positive:** Maintain a positive outlook, as setbacks are often temporary roadblocks leading to something better down the line.

Remember, closed doors are not endings but new beginnings in disguise. Embrace the journey, and you will find yourself opening doors to exciting possibilities ahead. Every chapter must come to an end to allow another new and exciting one to unfold. Trust that God has a divine plan. Live, learn and move forward – you've got this and God got you!

Chapter 5
Lauren-Ashley Heastie
"The Fast Track To Nowhere"

For most of my life, I felt as though I had some direction about who I wanted to be, where I wanted to go, and what my career would look like. I always imagined myself successful, passionate about my career and having the freedom to share my time in other civic activities and hobbies I enjoyed.

At this point in my life, not all of these dreams are fulfilled. To be honest, the life I imagined has not even fully taken shape. I guess you can say I am in that space where I can "tick off a few boxes" but I have not crossed over into my full dream. Sometimes, I feel like I am just living. Somewhere between working on the long-term goals but still too far away to fully grasp them. Honestly, that still sounds strange to me sometimes.

Being in my early thirties, I always thought I would have most of my life figured out by now, especially for my career, relationships, friends, education, or even myself. I am learning that life does not play out the way we design it to. In fact, life may never look the way we thought it would.

For instance, after I graduated from college with my Bachelors, I was overwhelmed with excitement. I finally felt as though I had reached the finish line and I was ready to stand on the winners' block for my medal. However, that feeling surely did not last long. It seemed as though my life had just come to a halt. Soon enough, I was in a dark cycle of TV shows and unanswered job ads, with no dream job in sight. Here I was filled with potential, enthusiasm, newfound knowledge and nowhere to utilize my qualities. I was stuck in limbo. Not really the dream I had in mind; and at this time, I truly had no answers. I did what I was supposed to do. So why wasn't it working? Where was my big break?

Eventually, my opportunity came. I was allowed to join a work program that exceeded my expectations by providing a welcoming and nurturing environment that changed my life. Anyone who knows me will tell you I have an introverted nature and I avoid the spotlight at all costs.

However, this job put me in front and centre! Whether it was for training or events, I learned to embrace "the centre stage," which still shocks me to this day. I was happy to see what this line of work brought out of me, but I was also concerned about this new transition. I think the fear of public opinion or even being in the public eye shook me. To this day, I am still not comfortable.

Through this transition, I have found that you will never see the true capacity of your potential if you do not take those small opportunities for growth. As a result, I now embrace change and relinquish repetitive habits that anchor me to the fear of change. My focus has expanded to the bigger picture and how I was helping to get the job done, no matter what it was. I truly became acclimated to the environment and, although it is fine just being a worker bee, this opportunity allowed me to hope for and want more. Being in such an environment that groomed me to expect the unexpected, I now have the confidence to do so.

I know you think this sounds pretty perfect, but the reality is a melancholy experience. The road to success can be quite long and the rest stops along the way do not seem rather rewarding. In this day and age, we millennials are looking for opportunities that grant us a flexible space to learn, shine, have a voice, and elevate without the humdrum "wait your turn" routine.

Well, here I am five years later and the "golden opportunity" I mentioned does not feel the same. Yes, the passion and the supportive working atmosphere are still there, but I want MORE and my expectation of more has expanded with varying requirements. With every year, we look to evolve and reach a new level. Sometimes our lives even make us feel like we have outgrown where we are and it feels like we are wandering in a dense fog until the path to our next step is visible. We all want to be ambitious and reach our peak as soon as possible, but the journey is not as fast-paced as we want it to be.

In some ways, our growth is stifled by the defects of the existing system that we call home. Let me tell you, there is nothing more frustrating than knowing that you can do great things, but you are being restricted by the very system that should aid you in your career. Do not let that discourage you. From my experience, patience pays off.

There were many days I felt weighted and discouraged by how the system did not play fair, and it hurt me especially witnessing how it impacted the very people I was employed to help, but paying attention to the broken system did not help me make a difference. I learned that regardless of the circumstances, you have to work with the system as closely as possible to override the experience for yourself.

I was blessed enough to be placed in a work environment that valued my opinion, gave me new opportunities, shared years of experience with me, and allowed me to take the lead on projects with little to no experience in the field. My supervisors embraced me and collaborated with me to raise me to the level they wanted me to be. That in itself is priceless!

Sometimes rewards can come in different packages. By embracing every new experience positively, we gain so much more. Yes, there were rough days, but eventually, it paid off. If I had kept my focus on how the system was not working for what I wanted, I would have missed some valuable lessons. It has also allowed me the opportunity to be in a more stable position to gain significant work experience and become a more well-rounded working professional.

Overcoming my low moments can still be a battle some days. Keeping focused on the positives helps me through those rough times. Getting sucked into a dark hole of comparison and disappointment is easy, especially when you start thinking about where you are and the plans you had.

Nowadays, it is so easy to feel left behind when you see everyone else achieving their goals. You start assessing your life, trying to figure out where you went wrong or what is missing. We are all guilty of playing this dangerous game at some point in time. But all it does is lead to distraction and kill your self-esteem.

I learned to combat these feelings by thinking more positively about myself and focusing more on what my goals were. When you are focused on improving yourself, you do not have time to worry about anyone else. By focusing on my strengths and progress, I prove to myself that I am great and I have promising things ahead of me.

My faith also keeps me grounded. Reading God's word and focusing on his promised plans for his children, I am immediately encouraged to stay the course. Yes, many trials may come, but the race is not for the swiftest.

Sometimes your journey to success will mean staying in one place and being patient. Take it from someone who is going through the process. These slow moments are the ones that will produce the greatest work as you are being pruned for what lies ahead. Take advantage of this time to improve yourself for what is to come.

As Nipsey Hussle said, "The marathon continues" and it does not stop. There is nothing more rewarding than seeing the fruits of your labour and knowing that you can share with someone else. I cannot wait to see what amazing journey lies ahead even if nothing much has changed. I know that my moment will come, and this waiting period will prepare me for bigger and better.

If you are like me and waiting for the train to your future destination, a little word of advice: do not watch the clock, just keep working and waiting. You are closer than you think.

Chapter 6
Sherell Brown

"In The Line Of Fire"

Having the ability to fight back and not being able to take strength is where I once found myself! The year was 2023, and we were still somewhat fresh out of a pandemic. The economy was struggling to rebound after three years of lockdowns, COVID-19 and a people grappling to find some sense of normalcy.

I was no different. See I am a serial entrepreneur and I occupy several spheres. One in particular is real estate - a field that I have a passion for; however, due to several reasons, my real estate was not generating the financial income that I had been accustomed to.

Firstly, the pandemic affected people's incomes, so finding people with stable salaries was a bit of a challenge and finding suitable tenants to meet the requirements for my short-term rental was another daunting task. As a result, it left me with a reduced income and vacancies at my rental property.

Then one day someone 'slid' into my direct messaging and inquired about my listing that I had posted on a popular site for people who were in the real estate market. The lady was cordial asking about the move-in fee and the requirements to move into the space. I obliged with the answers, and we exchanged cell numbers for further communication. But who knew that this was the beginning of the tenant from hell saga?

That initial encounter was the end of our exchange for a few weeks, then she 'slid' back into my chat inquiring if I still had any more spaces available for rent. I told her yes and that the requirement to move in was not limited to the amount to move in but also requested documentation such as proof of employment, police record, and a national identification card.

It was at this time she stated she was coming to Abaco, an island of The Bahamas, for work. She received a job offer at a bar, and this was the reason she needed a place to stay. I told her that employment was a requirement, but after she pleaded with me to rent her the space, my heart gave in.

See, I know what it is to not know where you are going to lay your head or where your next meal is coming from, so this made me very sensitive to her plight. I informed her that this room was one of my smaller rooms and I was currently still working on completing the renovations in the room. She stated that it did not matter; she just needed a place to stay. I told her in two weeks she would have a new mattress for the bed and the dresser was arriving from Nassau. However, she was still willing to stay in the space as is.

I remember what it was to have nothing and to start over. I know what it is to only need a helping hand. Against my better judgment, I allowed her to move in with no job and only on the word that she had sought employment. Silly me!

So, she transferred the required funds to my bank account, as policy would have it. With proof of payment and identification, she was allowed to move into one of my rentals. The first day she arrived, I confirmed the location of my rental home, and then she checked in.

The following morning, I messaged her to ask how she slept and if the room was clean and comfortable. At this point, she stated via text message it was and she slept great.

I then reassured her of the expected timeline for the furniture to arrive and that concluded our conversation. Two days later, I got a message from this young lady saying that she was desirous of returning to Nassau because she got her dream job offer and she would no longer be staying for the two-week period that she paid for.

I congratulated her on landing her "dream job" and then reminded her of our no refund policy as stated in the agreement. She stated at that time she had only been there three days and inquired as to why she could not be refunded.

At that time, I informed her that I was willing to return the security deposit once there was no damage to the space. She stated that she did not understand. I then stated to her that because her plans changed, same did not affect my policies and that also there was a cost of doing business.

I had to pay my house manager for services rendered just to prepare the space for her arrival. I removed the space from the market for other potential customers, so as a result of the expense I had already incurred, I could not refund because I would be operating at a loss. By this point, she was silent and I concluded the conversation.

The next morning, I awoke to a text message from my sister's cousin whom I did not speak to often, but for some reason, it was deleted. So, I messaged back inquiring about the text.

She then sent me a link and a screenshot of a post that was on Facebook. Same was trending. It had my photo and a secondary business name on it, with a comment implying that I stole her money and did not want to give it back.

Listen to me; I was livid! Heart pounding and belly breaking down, the stress was deafening. My mind was trying to comprehend what exactly was happening. My sister's cousin asked me if I knew Cassandra and I told her that she was the name of my new tenant. She told me to click on the link because she was on her page saying all sorts of bad things about me.

I, on the other end was flabbergasted. How did this situation that started with me trying to help someone result in me being an enemy or in this case a "thief?" Well, this was the beginning of eleven days of hell.

I quickly visited her Facebook page and read all the awful things that she was saying about me and the comments that were being posted underneath my business card flyer that had my photo on it. Comments from absolute strangers making fun of the situation, not knowing that she was only telling half of the story.

Someone once said, "A half-truth is still a complete lie." They were absolutely right. Now if you know me, I am saved, sanctified and filled with the Holy Ghost; but as a child of God, I was ready to "bust off this lady's head" for slandering my name.

Like how did we go from having a conversation about your request to slandering me in the public eye? Well, the reality was I was in Nassau and she was in Abaco, so I could not physically reach out and touch her, no matter how much I wanted to. But I definitely had some words of my own that I wanted to share publicly about this situation. I had determined to use my Facebook page to post about this young lady, the circumstances, and the course of action she had taken against me with her post.

I quickly reached out to my business partner and advised her as to what transpired and what I intended to do so that she would not be caught off guard when this post showed up on her news feed. It was in that instant that she told me these words that I will never forget, "TAKE IT DOWN." I was like, "What!!!!!" She said, "Yes, take it down." She also stated, "Do you know who you are? You are a businesswoman. You have thousands of followers and we currently have some big contracts on the table. You do not need to shed light before your audience on what this insignificant person is saying. You are now going to inform your thousands of followers of a matter that they may not even know exists and possibly harm your image or add fire to the flame."

But truth be told, I was ready to throw gasoline on that bad boy with a stick of dynamite and let the chips fall where they may. But I had more to lose by engaging in this social media scandal than to gain because I owed nobody an explanation and the people who really knew me knew that the person who was trying to defame my character was a liar.

After listening to the wise counsel I received, I deleted my post; however, it took the God in me not to fight fire with fire even though I was right, even though I had proof, voice notes, text messages, etc. My flesh wanted war, but for the sake of my character, my business, and my family, I had to choose peace.

Well, trying to make peace with my decision to choose peace was another fight altogether because when I tell you this girl tried to dig up the ant's nest, she surely did. She started taking photos of my home, more specifically of the room she rented and posting them on her timeline. The space that I told her was under renovation and she insisted on wanting the space. Now she was posting a photo to imply that I rented her something in a half-constructed unkept condition when I made her fully aware of what was happening.

This went on for about three or four days, then she went on to call me names, posted my personal photos, asked people to share my photos and message me on her behalf because at that point I had blocked her. She refused to remove the post, apologize, or see the reason. She also posted my mobile phone number publicly and asked people to call me on her behalf because she wanted her money back. Listen, the level of ignorance at that point was ridiculous.

While all of this was happening, she was still in my home using light, water and sleeping while living out the funds she paid to be there, but demanded it back at the same time. By this time, I realised this young lady "could not have been playing with a full deck of cards because the coo-coo was not on the clock." However, whether she was in her sound mind bore no weight or gave no solace for the demeaning and degrading situation I now found myself in.

Listen to all entrepreneurs and future entrepreneurs please remember not every client is your client. It is ok to walk away and say no. As much as a customer has rights, so do you - the product or service provider. Another thing I have determined is that this myth is a lie. The customer is not always right; however, they should always be heard and have an opportunity to voice their opinion. Do not allow them to dictate your decision on how to run your business and accommodate their requests.

By now I have been enduring this abuse for at least seven days, with no sign of letting up insight. So as a result, I consulted my attorney, who informed me that what she was doing was called slander and was not just an arrestable offense but was triable in the Supreme Court of The Bahamas.

She further stated that her service fee for matters of this nature was $300.00 an hour and should I desire to pursue her retainer fee was another $500. So, to initiate her involvement in this matter would have cost me almost $1,000.00. At this point, I was furious and felt helpless to defend myself, so I told her I did not care about the money; this was my name, and I was prepared to follow this through to the very end. She then advised me to first report the matter to the Central Detective Unit (CDU) to allow them to intervene before taking it to court.

The next day, I did just that and gathered all of my evidence and reported the matter to the CDU. Of course, I had to prove what I was saying, which I did, and an incident report was made. As a result, the Officer viewed the tenant's Facebook page, reviewed the postings and listened to the voice notes on my cell phone.

The Officer determined the tenant was in breach of the law. However, she insisted that we work this out of court because of the length of the process and it was a simple matter indeed.

I informed them that I attempted to, but this lady did not hear reason. It appeared as if she was enjoying the attention she was receiving from her Facebook followers and had no regard for my rights. They offered to call her to speak with her to attempt to bring a speedy resolution to this matter; however, they were unsuccessful.

At this point, they pointed out two considerations, one I was in Nassau and she was in my rental home in Abaco, and two that there was still a legal process of eviction I would have to go through should she not choose to leave willingly. At this point, I was questioning the law as to who it was protecting. Nevertheless, they asked me to allow them to reach out to the lady to attempt to bring a conclusion to this matter outside of court.

By now we were at day ten and the Facebook posts were taking a different direction. It was all about her crying on social media saying she just wants her money back so she can leave Abaco. By this point, I had contacted her boyfriend, whom she originally came to visit. She told him that I refused to give her the money back. I then stopped the young man in his tracks and updated him on everything that had transpired and validated that my position was not returning all of the funds, but reiterated that I was willing to return the security deposit as I had stated from the first day she made the request.

He then told me that what I said was not the story she told him and he apologized on her behalf and stated that she has to have money. That is why she wanted it back. She needed those funds so she could purchase a return ticket to Nassau. So, I told him my policy once again was security deposits are only returned after the person leaves the residence followed by the space being inspected. Once nothing is damaged or destroyed, we will transfer the funds to the account in which we receive the payment. I then suggested that he pay for her plane ticket to Nassau and he said that he would handle it.

Well, not even 24 good hours later, I got a call from the boyfriend saying that he was sorry I had to go through all of this. He viewed my profile on Facebook and saw that I was not into drama, but unfortunately, he and the lady broke up. I was shocked. "What do you mean broke up?" He said he worked on the Cay and took a ferry to visit her in Abaco. He tried to help her, but she was being very disgusting. They got into a fight at my home and she called the police on him and he left.

He said she was on her own and now had to find the money another way because he refused to help her. Well, look how the wind got knocked out of my sails. Here I thought, "Like thank you Lord, this is coming to an end, and now look, there is even more turbulence."

At this point, I knew she had no money, no food, no way of getting back to Nassau and she was stranded in my home with other tenants. Talk about a horrible situation.

I decided to update my husband on the latest changes in this situation and told him, "At this point, I am willing to go against my policy to get her out of my home by not just refunding the deposit before moving, but also sending it in cash because she had no way of receiving it."

He reiterated, "It was not your job to have to find a way to get her the funds." However, I told him, "It had become my problem because she was in my home and I just wanted her gone." So, he replied, "Do what you need to do at this point."

I contacted my Home Manager and gave her an update as to what transpired. She, like everyone else, was shocked. I then asked if I could transfer the funds to her and she take it to the rental home along with a document that she would have to sign confirming that she received the funds and would leave the home with no expectations of anything else.

She agreed and the next day confirmed receipt of the funds and letter and took it up to the house. Because she was the Home Manager, she had the master keys for the home and all of the rooms. I was informed that when she arrived at the home and entered, she knocked on the door of the room that was assigned to the lady and there was no answer.

She stated that she called out for her, which was when she heard a response from her. However, she was not coming from her assigned room. She was coming out of the room next door to hers and was standing in front of her in what she described as her birthday suit (barely any clothes). She stated that she told her to please put on clothes because she was there to bring her the funds and the document to sign.

She said, "The tenant got dressed and came out saying that she couldn't put me out and that she wanted her money." The Manager stated, "Didn't you call Mrs. Brown last night saying that once you got the money you will leave?" She said, "Yes, but she can't put me out."

I was informed that she picked up the phone in front of the Manager, called the police and said, "Mrs. Brown sent her home manager to put her out of the home and she is not going anywhere." At this point, my manager left to avoid further problems with this girl or the police. The

Home Manager called me and informed me of all she had just experienced and said the girl refused to take the money or sign the document. She stated, "She appeared to be very comfortable and looked to be living out of the room next to her."

I explained that "The room was occupied by a male roommate and she must now be in survival mode since she had no money, no food, no job and now no boyfriend." I then informed her that, "It was that roommate's phone that she used to call me off of the night before because I still had him blocked off of my phone because of the harassing text messages and phone calls."

My Home Manager then stated, "She could not be playing with a full deck of cards because she was standing there with the money and you now called the police after days of saying you want your money and all you want to do was leave." I told my manager, "She had been too comfortable. She appeared to be sleeping with the guy next door and now the immediate need to leave or survival mode was gone. Nevertheless, she was still a problem because she was still in my home and I did not want any damages or other issues arising because of her presence."

I kid you not, the next day I got a call from another roommate telling me that she was asleep and this girl came knocking on her window and woke her up out of her sleep to ask her to call me on her behalf. She said she asked her why. The lady said to ask Mrs. Brown to please send the house manager back to the house with the money cause she was ready to take it and go.

So, she stated, "Why didn't you take it yesterday? Mrs. Brown does not operate like that because she is cashless." She told her, "Mrs. Brown went out of her way to send the cash and got someone to bring it and you called the police." The tenant stated that she was tripping. She did not even know why she called the police, but she was ready now.

The roommate called me and relayed everything that she said and I told her, "No, I do not want to speak to you and no, the Home Manager cannot return. The Home Manager left her full-time government job to come to bring you funds that were contrary to her policy and you called the police on her."

Now buying her return ticket was her responsibility. I was done trying to assist her. She thought this was a game. Well, she learnt that I was not the one to play with. I hung up the phone which ended that conversation.

Once the lady had left, the roommate called me back and stated that she told her what I said and she started crying. Once again, she asked her why she did not take the money yesterday and she said she did not know.

Two days had passed when I got a message from the other roommate's phone saying that he was messaging on her behalf and she wanted me to know that she got someone to purchase her ticket and would be leaving Friday which was the following day if I could have the house manager check the house so that she can get her security deposit back. I told him, "Once it was confirmed that she and all of her belongings were gone, the inspection will be made and should there be no damage the funds will be transferred to whichever account she provided."

I then contacted CDU and informed them that she was supposedly coming to Nassau tomorrow so this would be the best time to communicate with her reference to the slander. Finally, I could almost see the light at the end of the tunnel.

That night, I had another conversation about all that I had endured with this citation for the last two weeks. Listen, this felt like the longest two weeks of my life. This whole situation started two days after she arrived and it's day fourteen.

She had officially lived out the two weeks that she paid for, whether voluntarily or involuntarily. She was now out of my home and after the inspection, no damage had been done.

So now the officer addressed the question of whether I would still be pursuing prosecution for all of the harassment and slander for the past 14 days. I told him I would pray on it and confirm tomorrow. The next day came, and I slept and prayed about the current situation that I was facing. I counted the cost, all that I had lost and what I could gain in procuring this lady who did not have $200 for a plane ticket. There was nothing she could do to undo all that she had done and financially, it would cost me far more than I could ever get in return, so I decided not to pursue it.

However, I was sure that the sun would rise. I knew that she was going to contact me when she had landed because she needed this money. As predicted, I received a phone call from an unknown number, which I looked at for a few moments before I answered.

When I picked up the phone, it was her and nothing had changed her tone and verbiage disrespectfully, so I hung up the phone. Click! She called in the same manner saying, "Mrs. Brown, you hung up the phone on me." I said, "Who do you think you are talking to? When you are ready to talk with sense, call back." Click! She called back a third time, this time in a calmer tone saying, "I only want my security deposit. I am here in Nassau. Can you send me my money? I will send you the account." I told her, "You can send me the account. I will screenshot proof of the transfer and this will happen once the inspection is completed by my Home Manager." She replied, "I had not checked it yet." I said, "No, you will do so when you get off from work." This ended our conversation.

After I ended that conversation, I contacted my husband and asked him to transfer the funds. He asked about the inspection. I told him, "The Home Manager could not make it until she got off, but I just wanted this over so I had the roommate check the room and send me a video." Nothing appeared to be damaged, so he transferred the funds and sent me the screenshot of the payment, which I sent to the number she was communicating from.

Listen, the way I cried when this was done, the way I prayed like Lord, why did I have to endure such an awful experience? But in the end, my response was worship and gratitude that he brought me out and through this situation.

I reflected on those fourteen days of hell this young lady put me through. She had me questioning myself. How did I go from trying to help someone make a fresh start to finding myself in the police station and discussing prosecution with my lawyer? Like, what kind of roller coaster ride I just got off?

Now one year later, life has come full circle. My real estate business is flourishing. I am a co-author of a book and I am using my story to help others while God gets the glory. So, if you are facing a tough situation, "that mess one day will be a message" and if you use strategy, that situation will benefit you in more ways than one (wink).

Lessons Learnt

1. One of the key lessons I learned was no matter how good your intentions are, someone with a bad character or evil heart would try to take advantage of you.

2. Another lesson I learned was do not compromise your standards or rules. The back of my contracts for tenants is filled with rules, regulations, and requirements designed to protect not just the tenant but myself. Despite those rules or requirements, I allowed my emotions to cloud my business judgment, and it cost me in the long run. Ensure that your business contracts are ironclad and that you have the controlling rights.

3. Another lesson learned was the power of wise counsel. My instant reaction to someone trying to publicly demean my character was to respond publicly. However, after seeking counsel and hearing wisdom, I learned that this type of response could do me more harm than good. If I had merely acted out of emotion, I could have caused myself as well and one of my businesses a major contract for acting in an unbecoming manner. No one likes a mess and God cannot bless it.

4. And last but not least, always consider the cost. If it could do you more harm than good, it is not worth it, or if you have more to lose than gain, do not do it. The sleepless nights, the frustration, the harassment, the phone calls, and everything I faced in my two-week encounter with this young woman was not worth a red penny I received for that rental and it would have caused me more in every sense of the word.

Chapter 7
Sandena Neely

"The Power of Being Pretty Extraordinary"

"Be more splendid. Be more extraordinary.
Use every moment to fill yourself up."
Oprah

My earliest memory from my childhood, growing up in the tiny, close-knit, yet impoverished community of Kemp Road, was one of an immense sense of belonging, love and hope beyond circumstances. My primary school years, winding summer days, cool and balmy December evenings all provided a platform for adventure, wonderment, and the possibilities of dreaming outside of myself.

Even before I came to know or found the language for it, I was on a journey to becoming pretty extraordinary. There may be readers who are 8, 18, 48 or 80 and it is my prayer that the words of this chapter, and this entire book, light, reignite or help you rediscover your passions and your innate strengths like never before.

The simple yet profound quote by Aunty "O" that marks the opening of this chapter has been a gracious guide to me for the past several years. I have found it to be a comfort, to be compelling and to be a constant.

I think of my journey to understanding the power I possessed to be more — to be extraordinary. It was not a journey taken in isolation, but in fact, it was garnered through relationships.

These relationships permitted me to come out of the cave I had been hiding in. They made me feel safe with the full embodiment of Sandena. They were not threatened by all I was. Those collective voices encouraged me to continue to take steps forward. This is an important process of incubation for all of us as we transition into our most extraordinary selves and in fact, encouraged me to be more me. They created the opportunity for the extraordinary parts to blossom and grow.

When I think of the word extraordinary, what comes to mind is my very own definition of the word which states that to be extraordinary is "to actually be ordinary, consistently and then finding ways to increase the margins of that order and colour it in a way that it becomes 'barely recognisable', as Master Motivational Speaker Lisa Nichols would put it." I became enthralled with the thought of being extraordinary and it led me to create the *Pretty Extraordinary Movement.*

The power of being "pretty extraordinary" comes to life through the acronym for the word pretty. One must be purposeful, resilient, extraordinary (of course), teachable, transformative and yieldable. The pursuit of purpose is one of the most common pursuits or journeys that people embark upon.

The late Dr. Myles Munroe popularized the quote, "The two most important days in a person's life is the day they were born and the day they find out why." To be in the pursuit of one's purpose gives meaning to life and enables us to establish the ordinary that we can then use to create the extraordinary.

I recall a time in my life, when I had barely made it out of high school, having only made the required GPA by 5 points or less, not being quite clear on the road ahead, and being less than hopeful, yet moving forward.

I enrolled in The Bahamas Baptist Community College, and the administrators and faculty saw qualities in me that I did not recognize in myself, so much so that they nominated me to participate in The Bahamas' National Youth in Parliament.

This was a defining moment in my life that marked a shift in my thought processes and gave me a decidedly different worldview and opinion of myself, far different from the story I was beginning to tell myself. A story where I could only see myself barely making an ordinary life and doing enough to just get by.

I am so grateful for the opportunities borne out of the will of those around me to step out on faith and give me a chance that I did not even think I deserved. It was an opportunity that shifted the trajectory of my life, from the ordinary to the extraordinary. The winding paths that would ensue and continue up to the present day are more remarkable than I can put into words. The contents of this chapter have been years in the making and are a gift to our collective future.

When one thinks of their passion, the thing that occupies their mind and their heart space, the thing that they would do without even being paid for it – this is how we identify purpose! This enables you to tap into your power and move forward with vigour and energy.

The power of resilience really lies in patterns. Who are you when tough calls need to be made? What can be expected of you? What is your track record? What are your values and daily disciplines that help to keep you mentally, spiritually, and physically strong? What are your practices? Core values? Habits? The 'Boost Your Personal Development' website lists 7 Personal Core Values of Phenomenally Resilient People as focus, flexibility, problem-solving, pragmatism, community, persistence, and self-awareness.

Power also resides in one's ability to be extraordinary. What this means is to take a picture of your life - your ordinary life and make it "more extra." The challenge is to take your capacity and expand it, expound upon it, do more than average, more than is expected, and come outside of yourself. Take a goal that you have set for yourself and ask these few questions – what makes it unforgettable, what adds that wow factor - you have to get absolutely cellular with this and make your goal and the achievement of it – pretty extraordinary!

There is much to be said in particular in this day and age about one being 'teachable,' coachable, having the capacity to be trained and mentored. Those who have harnessed the power of being pretty extraordinary continuously find themselves totally wrapped up in personal growth. To grow and to learn, one must first be teachable, and be fully embracing of the concepts of openness, transparency, and constructive feedback.

This is a journey without a destination. This causes one to evolve from dimension to dimension, when and as needed. As women, and other readers I am sure can also identify, we are often placed in positions where our evolution depends on the level and pace to which we are open to growing, finding the right teachers and our power and willingness to absorb.

I opened myself up to personal growth more than 2 decades ago when I realized there was so much more to learn outside of myself and that if I were to do so, I would need to submit myself to a lifetime of learning.

Personal growth requires confessing to yourself firstly, that your knowledge is limited and that you need to skillfully absorb information to be able to translate it to useful knowledge to leverage to your advantage. What started as an innocent journey has now turned into a full-scale intentional way of life.

My life is multilayered and multi-purpose in so many interesting ways. I submitted myself to deeper levels of personal growth a little under 10 years ago; I unwittingly took Transformational Speaker and Super Coach Valorie Burton on as my mentor. This morphed into me leaning in to, learning, and gleaning all that I could from her through her books and virtual teachings, and becoming an inaugural member of her Successful Women's Academy which she launched during the Covid-19 pandemic.

This mentorship deepened in 2023 when I decided to attend an in-person event where Valorie would be speaking. I made it my mission to meet the woman who had provided me with so much inspiration, guidance, and fuel. That dream became a reality as I courageously found a way to make my way out of the proverbial 'people pile' and meet my mentor.

It was another defining moment to connect with my Mentor who had meant so much to me, my transformation and my growth. It was an enriching experience and it served as a reminder to always be teachable and coachable.

The power of transformation in being pretty extraordinary is both underrated and groundbreaking. Transformation, although it can appear to be overnight, is really a progression that takes place with time and with meticulous, almost needling change, change that occurs with meaning and with subtle force.

The power of purpose, resilience, being extraordinary, teachable and yieldable all speaks to and results in massive transformation. Transformation is a granular process that when undertaken moves one from a cocoon phase to a butterfly phase, it is the most beautiful process.

This deepens for women who find themselves in a state of unknowing, which can feel dark and lonely but can actually place you in a position to spark something completely new, exciting and radically different from what you've known or experienced before.

Amassing a collection of experiences has the invaluable power to skillfully position you to have increased capacity and to prepare you for life outside of the ordinary, outside of the normal routine margins. Transformation takes on many different forms and has the power to usher you into the pretty extraordinary.

Being yieldable is the final rung of the pretty in the power of being pretty extraordinary. This is the final phase, yielding results is the mark of one who is pretty extraordinary. Statistics show that year-over-year people, on a wide scale, make annual goals and only very few successfully get past the first quarter of the year still on pace to achieve their goals.

Pretty extraordinary people gain momentum by the mere pursuit of their goals and they live in the overflow of the results. Being yieldable sets you apart from those who successfully achieve the mundane and the ordinary. Not only am I proud to state that I regularly meet and exceed my own goals – based on the pretty goals formula – it is my honour to share that I have an entire tribe of mentees who follow suit.

Being yieldable is important and for me, as much as I relish in celebrating or contemplating my own accomplishments, I am beyond thrilled and satisfied to know that I can make a wide-scale impact on those around me.

I am grateful for my support system in the way of mentors, my peers and yes, my beloved mentees. This brings being yieldable to an extraordinary level as I look at the kaleidoscope of mentees who range from educators, journalists, maritime professionals, educators, entrepreneurs, history makers, and exceptionally talented young men and women.

This chapter is in part, dedicated to them. I make certain that they are always aware that an overarching goal of theirs is not to be like or as good as their mentor. The goal is to be better, to do more, to reach further and to go higher, always.

Here is my view – everyone can be ordinary. We are not existing, living, thriving and growing to just remain the same. Our worldview and outlook should bring us the necessary satisfaction of achieving good success.

On the heels of the 50th Golden Jubilee Anniversary of the Independence of our great country, The Bahamas, I count it an honour to highlight the message of the Pretty Extraordinary movement, which women, and men, boys, and girls alike, can read and utilize as we march on to the next 50!

Chapter 8
Juliet Seymour

"You Are Worth It"
"An Unforgettable Story From My Life"

An unforgettable story from my life: I heard my name echoed across the shopping mall filled with people, "Girl, every time I see you, you are getting bigger and bigger." I felt as if the floors of the mall had opened up and swallowed me or I wished it did. It seemed as if every head in the mall turned in my direction to see who this "blimp" of a person was.

I vividly remember how humiliated I felt at that moment. You see, I had a flashback of my past as an overweight teenager and I remembered how that made me feel. Every ounce of self-esteem I had worked so hard to build went out the window in two seconds or less. Once again, I had allowed my toxic thinking, which we have all experienced at one point or another, to take over and overshadow my true beauty. I had always been insecure about my body and the way it looked, and the mall encounter exacerbated that.

Once again, I found myself craving to be what society coined *"beautiful."* I obsessed over my body's appearance. I picked at what was reflected in the mirror. I wanted others to not only admire my looks, but I cared what others thought about me and the reason was low self-worth. I felt inferior at the moment. I thought that I was inherently worthless not only because of what I looked like on the outside, but the inner work that needed to be done.

Because not being beautiful made me feel worthless compared to others - unworthy of a happy life, undeserving of a loving relationship and all the blessings that came with it and there was nothing I could do about it. Or so I thought.

So, I dedicated my life to the discovery of self-worth and showing other women how to make that same discovery. And again, society had some strict criteria to fulfil in order to be worthy of what I desired or deemed worthy - impressive possessions, qualifications, wealth, and other people's approval of worth. So did beauty. The more beautiful, flawless, and perfect a person is, the more worth they possess in society's eyes.

Instead of being grateful, I had allowed my mind to become conditioned and accepted society's version of beauty without questioning, but I had my own *ah-ha* moment. I am beautiful - period. As I searched for ways to truly love and accept myself, and in essence who I was as a person, I had another life-changing encounter with God and then I realised *and* accepted my body – all of it, in its beauty.

I take solace in the word of God that says, "I will praise thee; for I am fearfully and wonderfully made: marvellous are thy works; and that my soul knoweth right well." (Psalm 139:14) "Favour is deceitful, and beauty is vain; but a woman that feareth the Lord, she shall be praised." (Proverbs 31:30)

After these life-changing realisations, I was ready to embrace all of my beauty – inside and out. I went to work to improve my self-worth and break my mind's conditioning. After all, beauty is within all of us. Our body's outer appearance will change nothing about our worth or who we are. Our scars and imperfections cannot diminish our deservedness. Excess weight will not make us inferior to others, nor does it define who we are. We never were worthless. Nor will we ever be.

In discovering myself, I decided to release all of the negative self-doubt. I was introduced to a wellness company by the name of Ardysslife and in doing so, it helped me get healthier and it also helped me to lose over 100 lbs. By following one of their weight-loss plans, which included consuming nutritional all-natural products and reshaping not only my body but my mindset as well. As a result, I became an Independent Distributor of the company and now I am helping women all over the world to become healthier and change their lives one-step at a time.

There is a familiar quote that says, "She remembered who she was, and the game changed." I was more than my looks. You see, life was never about celebrating and finding beauty in where I was at every point in my unique journey. Life is not about *if* or *when* I lose weight. It is about the NOW. I realized that the true path to happiness was to embrace exactly where I was in my life. You must find happiness where you are right now.

Yes, getting to that point takes time. It is a series of baby steps marked by an intentional shift in attitude and mindset. Embrace you – embrace all of you – square your shoulders back, pull your core in, raise your head and shine in the space God has placed you.

To put it simply, you must find and embrace your beauty at every stage of your life and accept that you are perfect just as you are. You are more than your curves and edges. You are worth so much more. Until you find the courage to take this leap, you will never be happy. You will always feel inadequate. How is that for a reality check?

Finding ways to stand up to your own body-hate speech is so important. In order to embrace your body just the way it is, you have to start with the right mindset. What we think is what we become! When we apply self-compassion and self-love, our lives will change.

Sometimes the smallest things can make the biggest impact. These little exercises may seem small, but over time can help make a difference. Loving yourself is about finding happiness from the inside out.

Loving yourself from the inside out means embracing both your strengths and your flaws. Love your body and cherish it! If you are dissatisfied with yourself, love yourself enough to make the necessary changes to what you dislike about it.

Choose something you enjoy and something that will make you feel good about yourself. Exercise, get a hobby, write a book, volunteer your services for free, mentor a young women's group, cultivate your joy, cultivate your inner peace, and continue to build your confidence.

OK, you cannot specifically prepare yourself for every spontaneous experience that will happen in life. But you can prepare in a general way with a little pep self-talk.

For example, I might say, "You are beautiful and amazing exactly as you are." Then, I start listing all of the positives about myself so that I am not caught up in someone else's reality.

Your pep talk will be unique to you. Moreover, if you are really struggling, remember to start small. You might not immediately believe it if you say, "I am beautiful."

So, start with the small aspects that you see beauty in. Perhaps you have beautiful eyes or a beautiful smile – celebrate that.

Treat yourself every now and again. I also recommend going shopping for a few new pieces that make you feel good. Ignore the numbers on the clothing and go by how it makes you feel. It improves your confidence when you wear clothes that really fit you. Wear the proper undergarments and be sure to lift the girls high and whittle your middle.

You are a lady; you are beautiful and you are worth it!

Chapter 9
Jovita Charite

"Rising Above The Storm"

The Lord Nurses Them When They Are Sick
And Restores Them To Health
Psalms 41:3 NLT

The year 2020 proved to be a defining year in my life - a year that would forever be etched in my memory and affect the course of my life as I knew it.

On Friday, 10th April, 2020, my sister Jamila and I were both experiencing nasal congestion, which later developed into a fever. Being both nurses and before heading to bed, we decided to take medication with the expectation of awakening the following morning feeling much better. However, we both awakened to the same symptoms and, as a result, she contacted the Surveillance Unit Department of Public Health to report our symptoms. We did not want to take any chances, given that The Bahamas, like the rest of the world, we're dealing with the COVID-19 pandemic.

Later that evening, our father prepared supper. We ate and I went to bed. Shortly after, the Doctor called for an update on our condition and spoke with Jamila. Upon hearing the report, Doc stated she would call back in the morning.

The following morning, we received a call from the Doctor. While sitting, Jamila noticed I was breathing rapidly and decided to take my respiration rate. It was 44 breaths per minute (bpm). The normal range is 12 to 20 bmp.

She quickly ran to the room to get the pulse oximeter (an instrument that measures your oxygen level in the blood). My oxygen level was 78% at the time. Bear in mind the normal oxygen rate is 96 to 100%. Doc was informed, and she advised that we should go to the Princess Margaret Hospital (PMH) immediately.

Upon reaching our destination, Jamila realized that I was unable to walk from the parking lot and dropped me off at the front entrance. She parked the car and returned to give the nurse and doctor my medical history and to explain the symptoms that I was experiencing. I was then assessed and admitted for further evaluation and testing. We said our goodbyes, as she could not accompany me any further.

I was then taken into an isolated room that had a bed, a commode (substitute toilet), an IV pole, and a large oxygen tank. I was placed on 4L of oxygen via a nasal cannula and was given an IV access. As I sat in the isolation room, the night seemed as though it would never end. There was no clock to keep track of the time, nor was there a television to occupy my time. However, having them there would not have made a difference, because I was too focused on breathing. It was only God and me!

Throughout the night, I went from a nasal cannula to a non-rebreather mask, as my oxygen levels were drastically declining. My mother called to check up on me, as she would normally do. However, because of difficulty breathing, I was unable to converse with her. I could not understand how quickly things were escalating. I said to myself, "This could not be the same person who walked into the hospital just moments ago." Recognizing my struggle, my mom said, "Don't talk Joey, conserve your energy. I love you." My mom then prayed for me, placing me in God's hands before hanging up the phone.

Later that night, I felt the urge to use the bathroom. By this time, I was very weak and could barely breathe. I recall sitting on the edge of the bed and feeling faint. I could not call for help because there was no call button.

The next thing I remembered was lying on the floor with the commode and IV pole turned over. As I lay there and looked around, I said a prayer and asked for strength to make it back on the bed. My prayer was surely answered; however, I passed out again.

At some point, the Patient Care Technician (PCT) came into the room and noticed that the room was in disarray. He asked, "Did you injure yourself in any way?" I could not recall my response; however, he helped to reposition me comfortably in the bed and stated that the doctor would be in to see me shortly. Upon his arrival, he examined me and told me I would be swabbed for COVID.

Early in the morning, I was transported via a wheelchair to the ambulance that took me to the COVID-19 makeshift unit located outside of the hospital. A shoe covering was placed on my feet, and I was draped with a sheet during transfer. As I exited the ambulance, I started to feel faint again and was extremely weak. The Emergency Medical Technician (EMT) noticed that I could no longer maintain my own weight. Therefore, he called for assistance, and then I was quickly rushed inside. Once inside, I can recall them taking my oxygen level and stating that it was 48%. They quickly placed me back on oxygen.

The day did not go so well. I tossed and turned to find a comfortable position in bed. Even though I was receiving oxygen, my levels were declining instead of improving. Eventually, I was told that I had to be intubated. A strange doctor arrived to explain the procedure. Thereafter, my primary doctor came and spoke to me from behind the glass window (it then occurred to me that only one person could enter my room at any given time); "Ms. Charite, I am afraid I have some bad news. Your test came back positive for COVID-19." At that very moment, my heart dropped, and the spirit of despair started to creep in because all I heard before was that COVID was a death sentence and once persons were intubated, they died.

Immediately, I started to declare, "I shall live and not die" and repeated Isaiah 53:5 which states, "He was wounded for my transgressions and bruised for my iniquities. The chastisement of my peace was upon Him and by His stripes I am healed." The Doctor leaned in and asked what I said. I repeated myself and she asked if she could pray for me. I said yes, and she did. She encouraged me to get my phone and listen to worship music. She explained that because I was diagnosed positive, I would be transferred to Blake Road.

Later that night, I was transferred to Doctor's Hospital and admitted to the Intensive Care Unit (ICU) and the decision was made not to intubate me but to use a high-flow nasal cannula oxygen machine (a breathing support system that gives continuous, warmed and humidified oxygen through a tube that is placed in the nostrils. It is used when traditional oxygen therapy is not working, and it helps reduce the effort your body needs to put into breathing).

When I found out the next day that my sister was admitted, I cried because I did not want her to go through or feel what I was feeling. To turn in the bed, it felt as though I had just run a marathon. I was told that she was in the Medical Ward and not in the ICU. I stayed in the ICU for 6 weeks and during that time, they tried all the experimental drugs on me for COVID-19 and none seemed to work.

I remembered while lying in bed, my body was going through so much! I felt as though I would take one step forward, then ten steps back in a matter of a few hours. I was tired physically, emotionally, and mentally and I wanted to give up! I said, "God, I can't take this anymore. I'm tired!"

Right then the PCT came in and asked if I was a Christian. I answered, "Yes." "Then you should know that life and death are in the power of your tongue and that you must speak life and not death." It was just what I needed to be reminded of! So, I spoke life and said, "I shall live and not die."

A few days later the Doctor visited, and I asked him how many people in my situation recovered from COVID-19. He then told me that it was going to be a fight. I replied, "This is a fight that I am not going to lose, this will be my testimony because God has made some promises that have yet to be manifested in my life."

He responded, "Then let's fight!" At that moment, I was glad he answered with that response and did not tell me that I was the country's first critical case. His response encouraged me to fight optimistically and to trust in God.

Being hospitalised during this time was tough; not only because of what I was going through, but because I could not see my family. Even though we were both in the same hospital, Jamila and I could not see each other. Therefore, she would video call several times a day to ensure we used the spirometer together when we were supposed to, to ensure that I ate, and to practice our deep breathing exercises together.

My mother, father, grandmother, and Jamila would have devotions every night with me via video calls. Jamila stayed in hospital for three weeks and tears filled my eyes when she was discharged from the hospital. She told me not to cry and to stay strong, that she loves me and that she will be praying for me to be next. I told her that the tears were tears of joy because she was leaving. I was grateful that they allowed her to see me before she went home. She encouraged me to stay strong and that I would be home soon.

As I progressed, I was later transferred to the Medical Ward. This was great news! I thought, "I am one step closer to going home." However, a few days later, I felt a sharp sticking pain permeating from my knees down to the tip of my toes. You could not touch my feet because I would cry out in pain! A scan was done, and the tests revealed that I had blood clots in both legs in addition to my left arm. Because of this, I was placed on bed rest for two weeks to ensure that the clots did not dislodge and go to either my lungs or brain. Upon completion of bed rest, it was like I was learning to walk all over again. I began physiotherapy to assist me with strengthening my legs.

I was excited every day about going home. One month turned into two months, which then turned into three months. Finally, it was mid-July when I received the joyful news! However, they did not want me to have false expectations regarding my full recovery. I was informed that I had severe scarring in my lungs and that I would need to be discharged on oxygen. They could not predict the length of time that I would need it. But thanks be to God, I only used the oxygen concentrator machine for one week! My doctors could not believe it!

Before I left the hospital to go home, one of the Doctors shared that he would call me "Miracle" from this day forward because he witnessed a miracle in my recovery. He stated that death was at my door, but I did not let it in. If this was the reason for me to go through this ordeal, for one person to know that God is still a miracle worker, then so be it.

There were so many people here in The Bahamas and around the world who prayed for my sister and me. Colossians 1:9 says, "Be assured that from the day we heard of you, we never stopped praying for you." Acts 12: 5 states, "Constant prayer was offered to God for us by the church and the believers." James 5:16 says, "The effective, fervent prayer of a righteous man availeth much, it is dynamic and has tremendous power." For this, we are forever grateful. It was the power of prayer that brought us through and, like the Phoenix that rose out of the ashes, we rose and overcame.

Your storm may not be COVID-19. It may be your finances, relationships, finding your purpose, or health. Whatever it may be, I would like to say be encouraged, stand firm, and keep the faith. Put your trust in God and He will direct your path. During my stay in the hospital, in times when I was afraid, not knowing what would happen next, I knew that I was not alone. God was with me; He never left my side, and He taught me to trust Him. When it seems as if you are all alone, remember that God is only a prayer away. He promises never to leave us nor forsake us. He awaits patiently for us to invite Him into our hearts and allow Him to be a part of every aspect of our lives.

God's Word is full of golden nuggets.

Below are a few scripture references to encourage, strengthen, and assist you in rising out of the ashes, making a positive impact, and creating your legacy.

I leave you with these comforting scriptures:

1. **Isaiah 41:10** – God Will Strengthen You;

2. **Jeremiah 33:6** – God Heals;
3. **John 14:27** – God Gives You Peace;
4. **Matthew 11:28-30** – God Will Lighten Your Load;
5. **Jeremiah 29:11** – God Will Not Abandon You, He Has a Plan for You; and
6. **Philippians 4:13** – You Can Do All Things Through Christ Who Gives You Strength.

Chapter 10
Deborah Basden

"A Life of Legacy"
Humble Beginnings

My story began in a quaint little community on Abaco named Dundas Town. I was the third oldest child of thirteen, and the eldest girl. Helping my mother groom and raise my younger siblings was a daily task, and as an adult, I became aware that I was initially thrust into leadership, not necessarily by choice, but rather by obligation.

I could hear my mother's voice clearly as I got my siblings ready for school, "Deborah, did you feed the children, and did you pack their lunches?" To help with school preparation, I would wash all our uniforms on the weekend, iron them and put them away in the closet.

My mother was an amazing baker, just like my grandmother. She and I would wake up early every other morning before the sun came up to prepare bread so that my siblings and I would have fresh sandwiches for school every day. This was just one of my many responsibilities, and sometimes the pressure from all these responsibilities would bring me to tears.

Every afternoon I would look out the kitchen window at my friends playing in the street and wished I could join in with them. I just wanted to be a kid! There were days I wished I could get an extra hour of sleep and days when I would feel resentment for being the eldest girl.

My mother could often sense my hurt and would comfort me with a warm embrace, a kiss on my forehead, and a spoken blessing on my life. She reassured me that I was special, and she appreciated everything I did to help her with the family. It was not until much later in my life that I realized that though the experience was painful, it was all a part of God's plan.

The Shift

While attending choir practice at Dundas Town Church of God in 1974, I encountered the love of my life. He was a tall, handsome young man who was visiting from Nassau "The Big City". As he entered the sanctuary, we locked eyes immediately, I was shy and looked away, but I could feel his gaze the entire evening.

We started talking and time flew by. At the end of the evening, he looked deep into my eyes and told me that I would be his wife. I brushed off his comment with a nervous laugh and hurried home; however, he was serious. Over the next four years, he made frequent trips to Abaco to see me, along with bringing gifts. When he was not present, we would stay on the phone talking for hours. During this time, he would always ask me to be his wife, however, I felt as though I was too young. It was my mother and grandmother who told me he was a good man, and they were right.

Also, he was becoming so irresistible that I could not imagine life without him. So, on Christmas Day of 1978, we committed our lives to one another before God and our family. Shortly after, we decided to start our new life in Grand Bahama, The Bahamas.

On the career front, the insurance industry was booming, and I worked my way up to the manager of a prestigious agency. I loved meeting new people and travelling the world, but something was missing. The only time I would find true solace was when I was baking in the kitchen with my precious daughters.

We would make bread pudding every Saturday morning, and hot white bread to go with a pot of fresh pig feet sauce. This was our family's tradition. The more time we spent in the kitchen, the more I realized that I was not following my heart. I decided to make a plan. It was now or never.

I looked up to the heavens and whispered a small prayer:

"Lord I am afraid. I have never been on my own before, but please hear my heart today. By my 40th birthday, I would like to leave this job and open my own bakery. AMEN"

I went to work the next day determined. I set out a budgeting schedule and dedicated myself fully to the plan. Two months shy of my fortieth birthday, I placed my resignation letter on my director's desk and told him I would be moving on. He was disappointed and told me that I was giving up an awesome career with benefits to make bread. At that moment, I felt demeaned and insulted. This was the profession of my mother and my grandmother, our family's legacy. In this moment, I knew that I was prepared to prove him wrong, and anyone else who felt that way.

Soon after, fear began to creep in. Was I making the right decision? I consider myself a woman of great faith. I gave my life to the Lord at twelve years old and never looked back, but this was one of the most trying times in my life. I realized that I was going to have to do this, afraid.

A New Start

As a mother of five, I knew that my girls were depending on me, so I had to "show up" every day. I opened those bakery doors. At exactly 5 a.m., every morning, I would dedicate myself to spending time with the Lord. I would tell Him my fears, my goals, and anything that I needed to get off my chest.

I would pray over my products and ask Him to bless my customers. Things started slow, as most new businesses do. There were days I only made $20, but this did not last long. In no time my earnings surpassed that of my insurance job, and I was on the move.

My daughters began waking up early with me and would clean and grease the pans for the morning's bake. They would always tease me because truth be told, I never wanted girls. I wanted sons because I felt they were easier to protect; but again, God had a plan for my life from the very beginning and knew just what I needed.

Over time, I began to add to my bread selection. It was as if God was downloading recipes in my spirit. Whole wheat bread, raisin cinnamon bread, coconut bread, and the tourist's favourite, coconut swirl. Business grew so much that we had to relocate to a larger location, and this brought in new customers and new ideas.

The Legacy

At the age of 46, my husband quietly slipped into glory, leaving me with five young women to raise. He was my provider and biggest supporter, and this shook me to my core. These were very dark days for me and my girls. How do I go on when my whole world is gone and my heart is in a million pieces?

For many months, I laid in bed and refused to leave the house. My mother would stop by daily to bring me a warm meal and force me to eat. Nothing made sense to me anymore, and I could feel the spirit of depression engulfing me.

One day, my youngest daughter Chante came into my room, and asked "Mommy, are we going to be ok"? Suddenly, I was brought back to reality. Though I wanted to mourn my Winston forever, my daughters needed me. She was only 9 years old; she needed me.

I began a daily routine of morning praise and worship that lifted my spirit to push through. Reciting the word of God daily reminded me that I was not alone, and Abba Father still held me in his hands.

As time went on, life became easier as I watched my 5 girls grow up, go to university, and start new jobs and families. Looking at them now; young, successful, Christian women, I know that God orchestrated every part of my life through baking.

Those loaves of bread sent them to school, kept my lights on and continued to be a source of income for me. It also amazed me to see the love I have been able to share with my community over the years through my baking.

We have been able to feed so many hungry people and tell them about the Lord over the years through outreach. Proceeds from the bakery have helped so many worthy causes in the community and ministry. Nearest to my heart are the opportunities I am given to minister to other women in business who have experienced hardships; being able to encourage them that they will be alright.

I would always tell them to never give up. Business is not an overnight success. Stop chasing money and follow your dreams. It is an open door for helping others to survive. Get in touch with your creator, he knows the plans he has for you Jeremiah 29:11, "For I know the thoughts that I think toward you, saith the LORD, thoughts of peace, and not of evil, to give you an expected end." All things will work together for your good. Love what you do, for it is a heart thing. Oftentimes, pursuing your passion is so much bigger than you. Your obedience to follow God's plan for your life is connected to the destiny of so many others.

My girls are now at the helm of the family business, and I am excited to see where this new generation takes it in the future. Stay tuned for this is just the first of many chapters to come.

About The Authors

Acribba Lightbourne

AA

**Talk Show Host, Entrepreneur, Certified Life Coach
Counsellor, Minister of the Gospel**

Acribba Lightbourne's journey is a testament to the transformative power of faith in God. She has faced many life challenges, including abusive relationships, poor choices, brokenness, and infertility. Despite these setbacks, she connected with her purpose and emerged as a role model for women overcoming adversities.

In 2016, she birthed Finding Faith Ministries International, a platform to share her experiences and empower others to discover the true knowledge of God. In 2017, she began hosting Faith Talk, a weekly YouTube broadcast highlighting individuals who have overcome insurmountable adversities through faith. In 2018, she launched Faith Line, a clothing brand with faith-based messages that attract global clients.

In 2018, she appeared on the cover of L.O.S.E. Magazine, where her journey with infertility was featured, and in the March edition of She Is Light Magazine as a 2019 Girl Power Honouree, highlighting her as the "Oracle of Truth." She is the host of an annual Vision Board Party, biblically inspired by the scripture found in Habakkuk 2:2: "Write the vision and make it plain." Since 2022, she has led a prayer and Bible network, with members based in The Bahamas, Canada, Cuba, Europe, and the United States.

She is a wife, mother, certified Christian Life Coach, and a recent "honours" graduate from the Rig School of Apostles and Prophets' Masterclass. She also holds an Associate of Arts degree in Christian Leadership and Counselling from New Covenant University and is now pursuing a master's degree in Coaching, Mentorship, and Leadership at Edu Effective Business School.

Acribba is committed to community outreach programs and feeding the less fortunate. Her favourite mantra is "Prayer changes everything," and she is on a mission to win souls for the Kingdom of God.

Area of Expertise

Talk Show Host
Infertility Coach
Christian Leadership & Counselling
Mentorship
Minister of the Gospel
Community Outreach & Evangelism

For Bookings

Telephone: 242-359-1538
E-mail: acribba.lightbourne@gmail.com
Website: www.acribbalightbourne.com

Simmone L. Bowe
BA, MSc
Leadership Strategist & Consultant

Simmone is a seasoned, speaker, certified corporate trainer, personal development coach, HR strategist & consultant, leadership advisor, men's empowerment advocate, educator, mentor, newspaper columnist, soulful singer, and radio & television host. She was named a Caribbean Women to Watch in 2018 and was honoured as a Mentor of the Year by Project Bahamas in 2022. She has authored seven books.

Simmone has worked with small, medium, and large corporations in her areas of speciality and passion:

Shaping Vision & Strategy

- Facilitating executive and staff retreats (strategy & team building)
- Creating & Refining Company Philosophy and Cascading Vision & Goals
- Leadership Development

- Creating a Leadership Development Strategy
- Creating a Succession Planning Strategy
- Executive & Leadership Coaching
- Leadership Training Design & Facilitation
- Culture Transformation
- Conducting Research to Determine Root Causes for People Challenges (retention, engagement, morale, performance)
- Formulating Strategies to Address Root Causes & Providing Support to Implement in the Organization
- Improving Processes, Writing SOPs, Organization Design & Workflows
- Helping Executives Identify Cultural Direction and Partner to Create & Execute Strategic Transformation Campaigns

Simmone has a BA in English, a MSc in Career and Human Resource Development., and numerous certifications. Simmone has worked in both the public and private sectors, currently the founder and lead consultant of the boutique training and consulting firm Limitless Life.

Area of Expertise

Speaker

Certified Corporate Trainer

Personal Development Coach, Mentor

Limitless Life Leadership Strategist, HR Strategist & Consultant

Men's Empowerment Advocate

Newspaper Columnist

Soulful Singer, Radio & Television Hosts

For Bookings

Telephone: 242-557-8938

E-mail: Info@leadwithsimmone.com

LinkedIn: https://www.linkedin.com/in/simmonelbowe

Holly Riley-Woodside
BA, MA
School Principal, Entrepreneur, Mentor, Coach

Holly Riley Woodside, a native of Lowe Sound Andros, was born in April of 1982. A native of Andros, Holly or Icess, as she was so fondly called, grew up in the beautiful settlement of Lowe Sound.

Daughter of Vezel Evans and Genest Riley, Holly grew up with her extended family in the care of Vyomie Knowles, her adopted mother.

Holly is the mother of three children, Dionnete, Jonni, and John Jr. Holly's life centers around her family. She believes it is the backbone of most women. It gives them a reason to push harder, to not give up and to bear all.

As an educator with the Ministry of Education, she began her career as a Physical Education Teacher, after obtaining her Bachelor's in Education at The College of the Bahamas. In 2012, she completed her Master's degree from Kent State University.

She has worked in education for 19 years and has worked in primary and secondary schools. Holly worked four years as a subject coordinator, and three years as a senior assistant and has recently been promoted to Senior Mistress. She now serves as principal at Fresh Creek Primary School.

Creative, versatile, and passionate about her craft, she enjoys every opportunity to learn and to promote the personal and professional development of all around her.

However, In 2007 Holly was faced with one of the most challenging times, her daughter was diagnosed with cancer, and Holly travelled back and forth to Jackson Memorial Hospital where her daughter was being treated for cancer Now 17 years later, she is still being treated for chronic kidney failure.

This was a long and hard journey for her. The challenges financially, mentally, and physically nearly consumed her. There was not room to give up, to break down, or to fall apart. These were not an option. She had to always be strong. For her daughter to beat these chronic diseases, she had to stay strong, give her strength, keep her positive and happy.

Holly has a passion for the youth and their success. A teacher made a big difference during a difficult period in her life, and she wanted to be that to other young children. When asked why? She responded, "When I look into the faces of the children entrusted into my care, not only do I see my future, the future of my country, I see my kids, I see myself and I want the best for the youth, my kids, who are the future of my country. My future, our future depends on them!" Today, she credits her wide-ranging

Today, she credits her wide-ranging knowledge and education as the key to her success. Her analytical skills, innate creativity, passion, and love for work allow her to consistently reflect on the needs of those around her. She believes in teamwork and that each team member has something unique to contribute.

"Everything and everyone around you is your teacher." – Ken Keyes

Area of Expertise

Mentor & Coach

Educator

Youth Empowerment

Speaker (Girls & Young Women)

For Bookings

Telephone: 242-554-0552

E-mail: icess2882@hotmail.com

FB:

https://www.facebook.com/inkishcustomprinting?mibextid=LQQJ4d

IG: holly@inkishcustomprinting.com

TikTok: inkishcustomprinting242

Website: https://inkishcustomprinting.com

Sherry Johnson Deal
AA, BA, LIC, CYL, PMP, JP

**Diplomat, Empowerment Speaker,
CEO, Business Consultant & Investment Adviser,
Communications Expert, Certified Publisher,
Justice of the Peace, Certified Youth Leader**

Sherry Johnson Deal is a charismatic, humorous personality, and a valued resource in academic, personal, and professional circles for students, individuals, non-profits, religious, and community leaders looking to be empowered to go to the next level. Since her young adult years, she has not only studied the science of empowerment but mastered it by counselling, encouraging and coaching hundreds of young people in various leadership capacities.

As a former Junior Minister at a local church and National Youth Advisory Council Executive Member, Sherry inspires young people to meet the challenges of the world around them.

Academically, she has risen to the highest level of excellence, having completed secondary and tertiary level education with distinction (president's list and valedictorian awards). She holds an Associate of Arts Degree in Communication and Foreign Languages, a Bachelor's in Business Administration, Licenciatura in International Relations from prestigious Universities around the world. She also holds certifications in foreign exchange trading and project management.

Some notable achievements were in November 2019, she along with her team launched a not-for-profit organization named Purpose Path (Bahamas) International; and in January 2020, Ms. Johnson Deal graduated as valedictorian with distinction at the National Youth Leaders Certification Program Ceremony.

Professionally, she serves as a diplomat for the Government of the Commonwealth of The Bahamas. As the former United States and Canada Desks Officer, she has participated in countless high-level international and regional meetings where she represented the Government.

During her almost 14-year diplomatic tenure, she has served abroad in Atlanta, Miami, and New York. Currently, she serves as the Technical Advisor of the Bahamas Alrae Ramsay Institute of Foreign Affairs (BARIFA) within the Ministry of Foreign Affairs, The Bahamas.

Additionally, she is a member and The Bahamas point of contact for the African Women's Health Project International (AWHPI) headed by Princess Moradeun Ogunlana.

In 2022 and 2024, she was nominated as *The Marquis Who's Who in America*. In August 2022, she received the Top Female Millennial Award in the Commonwealth of The Bahamas because of her contributions to diplomacy, education and as a change agent.

Sherry can be described as a phenomenal woman possessing many talents. She is an entrepreneur, certified publisher, certified forex trader, best-selling author, and a highly sought-after empowerment speaker, Justice of the Peace, and business & investment consultant.

Her singular purpose is to assist people from all walks of life to discover and maximize their innate gifts, thus enabling them to achieve a sense of fulfillment. She strongly believes that dreams can become realities despite socio-economic challenges, setbacks and that by employing a thorough assessment of one's life, a course of action can be determined to guide one to success.

She is a living example that against all odds and with the right motivation, whether intrinsic or extrinsic, one can achieve their dreams!

Area of Expertise

Business & Religious Conferences & Workshops
Youth & Leadership Conferences & Workshop
Public Speaking Courses & Training
Leadership Training
Coaching & Mentorship
Business & Investment Advisement
Business Administration & Networking
Event Planning, Publishing
Citizens Security & Justice Crime & Violence Prevention Expert

For Bookings

Telephone: 242-557-8227, 917-936-1322, 242-828-0378
E-mails: sajohnsonglobalservices@gmail.com
distinctionpublishinghouse@gmail.com
purposepathbahamas@gmail.com
Websites: www.sajohnsonglobalservices.com
www.distinctionpublishinghouse.com.
www.purposepathbahamas.org
IG: @sherryjempowermentspeaker
LinkedIn: https://www.linkedin.com/in/sajohnsonglobal

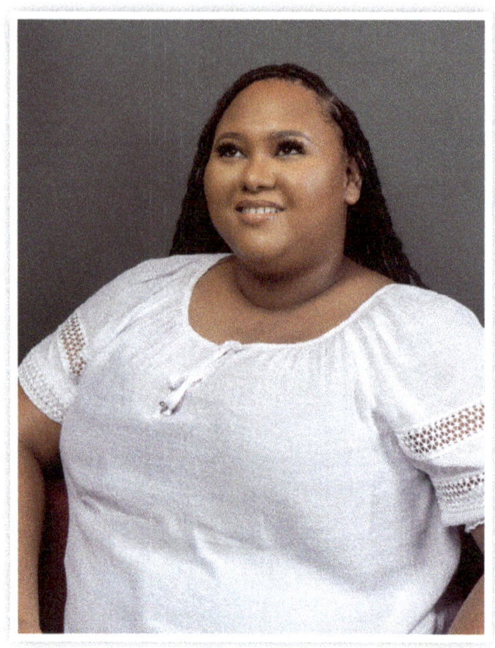

Lauren-Ashley Heastie
BA, MSc, CYL

Certified Youth Leader, Counsellor, Club 7773041 Toastmaster, Red Cross Society Volunteer, Kappa Delta Sigma Graduate Chapter of Sigma Gamma Rho Sorority Incorporated

Lauren-Ashley Heastie is an Administrative Cadet employed within the Ministry of Youth Sports and Culture where she facilitates, creates and manages programs and activities that help to positively impact the lives of Bahamian youth. With a passion for helping others, Lauren-Ashley obtained her Bachelor's degree in Psychology and is currently pursuing her Master's in Clinical Mental Health Counselling at Barry University. Upon completion of her studies, she hopes to further her career in Addiction and Individual Counselling.

Lauren-Ashley's passion for helping others also sparked a spirit of volunteerism and advocacy. She is a member of various civic organizations such as Kappa Delta Sigma Graduate Chapter of Sigma Gamma Rho Sorority Incorporated, Club 7773041 Pinewood Trendsetters Toastmasters Club, and The Bahamas Red Cross Society.

In her free time, she loves travelling, movies, the beach, and a good book. Lauren-Ashley hopes that through her dedication to service to the mental health industry and youth engagement, she will help propel the mission of both fields in The Bahamas.

Area of Expertise

Youth Leadership & Development

Mental Health Counsellor

Mentorship & Coaching

Digital Application Specialist

Speaker

Citizens Security & Justice Crime & Violence Prevention Expert

Trauma-Informed Care Expert

For Bookings

Telephone: 242-449.4148

E-mail: laheastie@gmail.com

LinkedIn:

https://www.linkedin.com/in/lauren-ashley-heastie-52028853/

Sherell Brown
AA, CYL

**Serial Entrepreneur,
Media Personality, Certified Publisher,
3x Amazon Best-Selling Author in Multiple Categories, Speaker
Certified National Youth Leader**

Sherell Brown is a former member of the Royal Bahamas Police Force where she served for 15 years in different capacities; however, the bulk of her service was spent in the Central Detective Unit (CDU) where she investigated major crimes. Her 15-year tenure ended in 2015.

She then pursued a career in Media, where she uncovered her passion for Radio, Journalism, and the Performing Arts. From this career move, Brown Inc. Production and Entertainment Studios was born. Since then, Sherell has produced several shows such as *Real Talk With Sherell*, a live online show that can be viewed or listened to on SoundCloud, YouTube, and Facebook.

Sherell is the former host of Ask Sherell and is currently still producing a weekly podcast where people can tune in from all over the world. Sherell gained her hands-on experience from working at Radio Abaco 93.5 and from hosting her own talk show at Shout 93.9 FM, formerly known as "Lady Rellz".

If there is an event happening, Sherell can be found behind the microphone, as she is nicknamed "the voice". She is also a registered voice-over talent with ACX, a subsidiary of Amazon, where she is a narrator for Audio Books. Sherell, the CEO of Brown Inc. Production & Entertainment Studios, Publisher of "L.O.S.E" Health & Wellness Magazine, and Co-Partner of Distinction Publishing House in Dover, Denver, Colorado. Sherell is a three (3) times best-selling author, having authored The Blueprint To Weight Loss The Truth Revealed, Lifting The Weight, The Journey to Total Freedom, and the best-selling Co-Author of The Woman Behind The Mask.

Sherell Brown is an Author, Speaker, Radio Personality, International Speaker, Producer, Narrator, and Performer. She has an Associate Degree in Human Resource Management and is continuing to pursue tertiary-level education. Sherell lives in Nassau, The Bahamas with her husband Desmond Brown and her four children: Seth, Grace, Samiya, and Simon Brown.

Area of Expertise

Event Hosting
Publishing Services
Entrepreneurial Talks
Speaker for Church Conferences, Workshops, Graduations
Citizens Security & Justice Crime & Violence Prevention Expert

For Bookings

Telephone: 242-819-7991
E-mail: sherellbrown1302@gmail.com
FB: https://www.facebook.com/sherell.brown.98
https://www.facebook.com/distinctionpublishinghouse
IG: sherell.e.brown,
TikTok: busy.body.brown.b
Website: www.distinctionpublishinghouse.com
Website: www.purposepathbahamas.org

Sandena O. Neely
LLB, LEC
**Consultant, Attorney, Coach, Mentor,
Youth Director, Speaker, Author**

Sandena Neely is a multi-dimensional leader who serves from the reservoir that God has gifted her. She is a very proud graduate of Uriah McPhee Primary School, St. Augustine's College, Bahamas Baptist Community College, University of the West Indies and finally, the Eugene Dupuch Law School. She sees herself as continuing evidence that something good can come out of the Kemp Road community. She seeks to nurture the rich culture, pastimes, and traditions from her early years and connect them to the diverse groupings of people in today's society.

She is an Attorney with 17 years of Call to the Bar and was proud to serve as an Associate Legal Counsel with the Atlantis Resort and Casino, Paradise Island from 2013 to 2019.

In October 2019, Sandena experienced a full circle moment when she made a career transition and left the legal field to accept a national assignment as a consultant with the Ministry of Youth, Sports and Culture. She has an invaluable support system in her two children, amazing parents, siblings, and a network of close friends. Sandena and her family worship at Revolution Church, where she serves as the Lead for the Public Relations and Guest Relations Ministries.

Sandena is the Founder and CEO of the Pretty Extraordinary movement and is passionate about personal growth and desires to see people lead extraordinary lives. Through this movement, she serves her community as a consultant, coach, mentor, thought-shifting speaker and author. On Tuesdays, Sandena leads her weekly Fierce Forty Prayer Call, designed to cultivate deeper and more enriching prayer lives. She is also an avid Dallas Cowboys fan!

Area of Expertise

Conferences & Workshops
Strategic Consultancy
Legal Advisement
Leadership Training
3, 6, 12 Month Life Planning
Pretty Extraordinary Talks

For Bookings

Telephone: 242-424-4137
E-mail: sandenaneely@gmail.com
Website: www.sandenaoneely.com

Juliet Seymour
BA
Ordained Minister, Certified Etiquette Coach
Mentor, Business Administrator, Entrepreneur
President at ArdyssLife

Lady Ju, as she is affectionately called, is a woman of great strength, honour, and integrity who serves passionately and with a spirit of excellence. She is an ordained minister and an eloquent example of a Godly woman. She considers her family her first ministry.

She is an administrator by profession. She is also a Certified Etiquette Coach and President at Ardyss International, a health and wellness company. "Don't blend in, stand out" and "Excellence without exception" are her mottos.

Her gift has made room for her, allowing her to minister nationally and internationally at various retreats, conferences, marriage seminars, seminars, and workshops.

She enjoys reading, writing, baking and travelling.

Area of Expertise

Ordained Minister

Certified Etiquette Coach

Mentor

Business Administrator

Entrepreneur

President at ArdyssLife

Speaker International Conferences & Workshops

For Bookings

Telephone: 242-554-0595

E-mail: julietseymour@hotmail.com

FB: Juliet Sunshine Seymour

IG: Julietseymour (JulietMaxi)

TikTok: @Julietsunshinesey

LinkedIn: Linkedin.com/in/Juliet Seymour

Jovita Charite
A.A., B.S.N, R.N.

**Computer Electronics Specialist, Nurse, Patient Care Technician,
Leader, Distinguished President Kiwanis (2019 – 2020),
Trained in Disaster Management
International Medical Mission's Group Volunteer**

Jovita Charite was born in Freeport, Grand Bahama, and relocated to Nassau as a child, where she continued her primary and tertiary education. Upon completion of high school, she enrolled in Atlantic Technical College and graduated with a Technical Diploma in Computer Electronics. After graduation, she gained employment with Broward County Animal Care and Regulation as a Computer Data Processor in Florida.

As Nursing was still on her mind, and in pursuit of her passion, she embarked on the journey to gain the skills and knowledge needed by enrolling in Hillsborough Community College, where she obtained her Associate of Science Degree in 2010.

She later transferred to South Dakota State University and completed her Bachelor of Science Degree in Nursing in 2015. Jovita had always found herself embracing the opportunities to help those she encountered. Hence, her decision to venture into a field embodying just that was no surprise to her family and friends.

Jovita has received several awards such as Most Outstanding Student Award for the Patient Care Technician Course, being on the 2014 – 2015 Dean's List, The 2004 – 2005 United Who's Who Registry for Executive and Professionals Award, Chairman Award for Leadership, 2018 – 2019 Kiwanian of the Year for Central Abaco, 2019 – 2020 Outstanding Leadership Award from Kiwanis Division, 2019 – 2020 Leadership Award from the Kiwanis Club of Central Abaco for Outstanding Leadership and Contributions to the organization.

With such a bubbly and contagious personality, this enabled her to explore various jobs such as working at Angel Health Care Agency in Florida, Doctor's Hospital in Nassau, Bahamas, Interim Health Care in South Dakota, and Integrated Medical Centre in Abaco, Bahamas. As a nurse, she is BLS and ACLS Certified with training in Disaster Management.

Nurse Charite's communication style is easy-going, which allows her to communicate with her patients well. When she is not working, you can find her lending her time, talents, and treasures volunteering with various organizations. Most recently, she demonstrated these key values by volunteering in May 2023 to travel to Kenya, along with a mission group to provide medical assistance to residents of the surrounding villages.

She stands firm in her beliefs and her favourite scriptures are Philippians 4:13, "I can do all things through Christ who gives me the strength," and Luke 1:37, "For with God nothing shall be impossible."

Area of Expertise

Computer Electronics Specialist
Training in Patient Care
Training in Disaster Management
International Medical Volunteer

For Bookings

Telephone: 242-818-6707 / 242-475-5028
E-mail: charitejovita@gmail.com
FB: https://www.facebook.com/jovita.charite?mibextid=ZbWKwL

Deborah Basden

Entrepreneur, Christian Minister

Deborah Basden, owner of Bahamas Tastiest Bakery, formally Da Bes Yet Bakery, was born and raised in Dundas Town, Abaco, Bahamas. She is the daughter of Delgarno and Viola Newbold. She obtained her primary education from Dundas Town Primary School and then her high school diploma from Abaco Central Secondary.

For most of her early career, Deborah has been in the insurance field, however, she decided to go full time into her passion, baking. Da Best Yet Bakery was established and has been nothing but successful over the years.

Deborah has had the opportunity to meet so many people, whether it is locals or tourists, who always come looking for her special baked goods.

Because of her vibrant personality, she and her bakery were featured on the HGTV show Caribbean Life.

In 2019, after the horrifying impact of Hurricane Dorian, Deborah had to close her bakery after losing everything in the storm; however, that did not stop her from doing what she loved. She started to bake once again from her home, which then led to her re-opening her shop front. The bakery was renamed Bahamas Tastiest Bakery.

Deborah was married for twenty-seven years to the love of her life, Keith Basden, until his demise in 2005. This union produced five beautiful daughters: Carol, Christina, Cinquetta, Claire, and Chante. She also has four grandchildren: Christopher, Kaleya, Jordyn, and Christian.

Deborah is a devout Christian who loves the Lord. She grew up attending the Methodist church and then The Church of God with her family. There she took ministerial classes, where she became a preacher and teacher alongside her husband. If you ever cross her path, she will always encourage you in the things of the Lord.

Area of Expertise

Entrepreneur
Christian Leadership & Counselling
Minister of the Gospel
Community Outreach & Evangelism

For Bookings

Telephone: 242-815-8847
E-mail: debbiec.basden@hotmail.com